The Tiger's Pretend Husband

Shifters of Rawr County, Volume 5

Sophie Stern

Published by Sophie Stern, 2022.

This is a work of fiction. Similarities to real people, places, or events are entirely coincidental.

THE TIGER'S PRETEND HUSBAND

First edition. May 16, 2022.

Copyright © 2022 Sophie Stern.

Written by Sophie Stern.

Also by Sophie Stern

Alien Chaos
Destroyed
Guarded
Saved
Christmas on Chaos
Alien Chaos: A Sci-Fi Alien Romance Bundle

Aliens of Malum
Deceived: An Alien Brides Romance
Betrayed: An Alien Brides Romance
Fallen: An Alien Brides Romance
Captured: An Alien Brides Romance
Regret
Crazed
For Keeps
Rotten: An Alien Brides Romance

Anchored
Starboard
Battleship
All Aboard
Abandon Ship
Below Deck
Crossing the Line
Anchored: Books 1-3
Anchored: Books 4-6

Ashton Sweets
Christmas Sugar Rush
Valentine's Sugar Rush
St. Patty's Sugar Rush
Halloween Sugar Rush

Bullies of Crescent Academy
You Suck
Troublemaker
Jaded

Club Kitten Dancers
Move

Pose
Climb

Dragon Enchanted
Hidden Mage
Hidden Captive
Hidden Curse

Dragon Isle
The Dragon Fighter
A Dragon's Bite
Lost to the Dragon
Beware of Dragons
Cowboy Dragon
Dark Heart of the Dragon
Once Upon a Dragon
Catching the Dragon

Fate High School
You Wish: A High School Reverse Harem Romance
Freak: A Reverse Harem High School Romance
Get Lost: A Reverse Harem Romance

Good Boys and Millionaires
Good Boys and Millionaires 1
Good Boys and Millionaires 2

Grimalkin Needs Brides
Ekpen (Intergalactic Dating Agency)

Honeypot Babies
The Polar Bear's Baby
The Jaguar's Baby
The Tiger's Baby

Honeypot Darlings
The Bear's Virgin Darling
The Bear's Virgin Mate
The Bear's Virgin Bride

Office Gentlemen
Ben From Accounting

Polar Bears of the Air Force
Staff Sergeant Polar Bear
Master Sergeant Polar Bear
Airman Polar Bear
Senior Airman Polar Bear

Red
Red: Into the Dark
Red: Through the Dark
Red: Beyond the Dark

Return to Dragon Isle
Dragons Are Forever
Dragon Crushed: An Enemies-to-Lovers Paranormal Romance
Dragon's Hex
Dragon's Gain
Dragon's Rush: An Enemies-to-Lovers Paranormal Romance

Shifters at Law
Wolf Case
Bearly Legal
Tiger Clause
Sergeant Bear

Dragon Law

Shifters of Rawr County
The Polar Bear's Fake Mate
The Lion's Fake Wife
The Tiger's Fake Date
The Wolf's Pretend Mate
The Tiger's Pretend Husband
The Dragon's Fake Fiancée

Stormy Mountain Bears
The Lumberjack's Baby Bear
The Writer's Baby Bear
The Mountain Man's Baby Bears

Sweet Nightmares
The Vampire's Melody
The Sound of Roses

Team Shifter
Bears VS Wolves
No Fox Given

The Fablestone Clan
Dragon's Oath
Dragon's Breath
Dragon's Darling
Dragon's Whisper
Dragon's Magic

The Feisty Dragons
Untamed Dragon
Naughty Dragon
Monster Dragon

The Hidden Planet
Vanquished
Outlaw
Conquered

The Wolfe City Pack
The Wolf's Darling
The Wolf's Mate
The Wolf's Bride

Standalone
Saucy Devil
Billionaire on Top
Jurassic Submissive
The Editor
Alien Beast
Snow White and the Wolves
Kissing the Billionaire
Wild
Alien Dragon
The Royal Her
Be My Tiger
Alien Monster
The Luck of the Wolves
Honeypot Babies Omnibus Edition
Honeypot Darlings: Omnibus Edition
Red: The Complete Trilogy
The Swan's Mate
The Feisty Librarian
Polar Bears of the Air Force
Wild Goose Chase
Star Princess
The Virgin and the Lumberjacks
Resting Bear Face
I Dare You, King
Shifters at Law
Pretty Little Fairies
Seized by the Dragon

The Fablestone Clan: A Paranormal Dragon-Shifter Romance Collection
Star Kissed
Big Bad Academy
Club Kitten Omnibus
Stormy Mountain Bears: The Complete Collection
Bitten by the Vampires
Beautiful Villain
Dark Favors
Savored
Vampire Kiss
Chaotic Wild: A Vampire Romance
Bitten
Heartless
The Dragon's Christmas Treasure
Out of the Woods
Bullies of Crescent Academy
Craving You: A Contemporary Romance Collection
Chasing Whiskey
The Hidden Planet Trilogy
The Bratty Dom
Tokyo Wolf
The Single Dad Who Stole My Heart
Free For Him
The Feline Gaze
Fate High School
Dragon Beast: A Beauty and the Beast Retelling
Boulder Bear
Megan Slays Vampires
Once Upon a Shift: A Paranormal Romantic Comedy

She needs protection.
He needs a plan.
Darla isn't exactly a tiny person. In fact, she's more than a person. She's a tiger shifter. Still, her kitty-cat claws are no match for the people who are hunting her. She crossed the wrong people one too many times, and now they're after her.
But Darla has a plan.
What she needs, more than anything else, is protection. What she wants, more than anything else, is Kapono.
Will he agree to marry her to keep her safe?
He may be able to protect her body, but can he protect her heart?

1

Darla

He was tall.

That was the thing I noticed about the man with the leather jacket as I stood before him in his bar.

He was tall, and he made me feel tiny.

That wasn't good.

I'd been made to feel small my entire life. I'd been tricked into feeling tiny. Now the very last thing in the world I wanted was to feel small and insignificant and teeny.

There I was, though: feeling it.

"Are you Jim?" I asked him. The woman at the diner had told me about this man. He was the one who was supposed to help me. He ran this little bar in Wishville, which was a place in Rawr County. It wasn't exactly far from Honeypot, but it wasn't just around the bend, either. I'd spent a couple of hours driving, which was long enough for my car to stop working twice. I'd been tempted to shift into my tiger form and run the rest of the way, but if I'd done that, I would have arrived naked, sweaty, and without any sort of identification or personal belongings.

My plan for survival wasn't going to work very well if I couldn't find anyone to offer me shelter.

The man glanced up at me from where he was wiping down the counter. He didn't seem very friendly. He hadn't said hello to me and he hadn't seemed very interested in the fact that I was there.

So, was he the one I had been looking for?

"Who's asking?"

"I am."

Irritation welled up within me. Georgia didn't say he was annoying: just that he'd give me a place to stay. They were old friends of some sort. He'd grown up near her, I guess. I'd met her quite by accident and she'd known instantly that I was in trouble. Maybe it was too much to think that this guy would be willing to help me.

Space.

I needed space.

I had to find a place where I could just *be*. I'd been running from Dwayne and his business partner, Mike, for nearly two weeks. They weren't going to let me go, though. Not forever. I didn't want to spend the rest of my life running, but if I could make myself disappear...if I could form a life somewhere...then everything would be okay.

Wouldn't it?

"Look." The man placed his hands on the faded bar counter. I had no idea how old this place was. It certainly wasn't new. Definitely wasn't like anyplace I'd ever seen. It had sort-of a rustic, dive-bar kind of feel: complete with dickish bartender. "I don't have time for your attitude. What the hell do you want?"

I glared at him.

What did I want?

I wanted a fucking break.

That was what I wanted.

I wanted two days where I could stay in the same place and not have to worry about looking over my shoulder. I wanted some time where I didn't feel like I was being stared at like a total freak. I wanted to be able to walk into a store and not feel nervous that the people in the next aisles were after me in any sort of way.

That was what I wanted.

It seemed as though I wasn't going to get it, though.

Instead, I was stuck dealing with Georgia's "friend" who wasn't very much of a friend. I had been sure she had called ahead to let Jim know I was coming. That was kind of part of the deal. She was going to let him know and then I was going to show up and start working at the bar. At least, that was what I'd hoped for. Georgia had promised only that Jim might be able to let me stay for a little while, and unlike Honeypot, it was big enough that I might be able to blend in for a little while.

Honeypot was nothing more than a blip on the highway. It was the epitome of "small town." While Rawr County was a bigger place, it had little pockets that felt smaller and close-knit. A few of the towns within the county were tiny, like Wishville was, but others were larger cities complete with high rise buildings.

The bar we were standing in was just a normal, run-of-the-mill brick building that probably had a moldy basement and a dilapidated apartment upstairs.

Who knew?

Maybe this guy would let me throw a sleeping bag up there so I could rest my head for a bit.

It was starting to look like Georgia had been wrong, though. I was beginning to get the distinct impression that whatever happened next was not going to be very fun at all. He was going to boot me out, I realized.

Then what was I supposed to do?

Anger welled up within me and I forgot about being nice.

"Georgia told me you were a nice man. She didn't warn me that you were a complete asshole," I snapped.

There.

I'd done it.

I'd told him what for.

Only, this guy wasn't the type of man who was going to take that sort of disrespect.

His hand shot out and he gripped my throat. His eyes narrowed and he tightened his grasp on my skin.

What.

The.

Hell?

Who the hell did this guy think he was?

He was *choking* me just because I'd had the balls to stand up to him. Well, tough. Too bad for him. If he didn't like girls who talked back, then he shouldn't be hanging out in this dumb bar!

"Let go!"

He didn't move.

He didn't seem at all bothered. Reaching up, I started flicking his fingers.

"Let go of me!"

He wasn't gripping me hard enough to do any real damage. It was just enough to be annoying. Still, I didn't want to be here all night. I definitely didn't want to be here being choked by this monster of a man.

At least, not like this. If I was going to be *choked* by a guy like this, then I'd want it to be in bed. I'd want it to be in a way that made me feel dirty and wild and free.

I wanted it to be in a way that made me feel *bad*.

This?

This didn't feel naughty or sexy.

It just felt annoying.

"Let me go!"

He sighed as though I was encroaching on his time. That was really the most irritating thing of all.

"Listen up, little girl."

"I'm not a little girl! Get your fucking hands off me!"

I slapped at his hand again, hoping he'd take the hint and finally let me go. Unfortunately for me, he did not. Instead, he just yawned, as though he had all the time in the world.

As though this wasn't bothering him.

"Fuck you! Let me go."

It was the disrespect that he really seemed to hate. He didn't mind me wiggling. He didn't mind me trying to wrestle myself free. There was an entire bar between us, but that didn't seem to matter. I was on the "customer" side of the bar and he was on the employee side, but his grip held firm. Licking his lips, he spoke again.

"If you come into my bar and throw a tantrum like a little girl, I'm going to call you a little girl."

Then he growled.

He growled at me.

Who the hell did he think he was?

"I'm going to let go of you and you're going to find some manners real fucking quick or you can get the hell out of here."

So that was it.

He wanted me to be polite.

He dropped his hand from my throat and tugged his cell phone out of his back pocket. His jeans were too tight. Even from my position on the other side of the bar, I could see just how the jeans worked like a second skin for him. I thought only girls liked wearing jeans that tightly. Apparently, I was wrong.

He punched in a couple of things and then waited. He held the phone to his ear but his eyes were on me. I rubbed at my throat dramatically, hoping that acting like I was in pain – I wasn't – would be enough to make him feel bad.

Something told me that I wasn't the first woman he'd choked. I definitely wouldn't be the last.

"Yeah. Georgia? It's me. Yeah, I'm good."

I stared at him. He was calling her on the phone. Why? Why was he doing that?

"How's everyone doing? Family doing okay?"

He waited. He was talking to her, but he was staring at me. I didn't move. It was this intense sort of gaze that made me feel like I had done something wrong even though I definitely hadn't. What the heck? Why was he looking at me like this?

"Good to hear. Good to hear all of that." He nodded as he spoke, and I had the distinct impression that this really was an old friend. I wasn't sure just how far back the two of them went, but it seemed to be at least a little ways.

I looked around the bar as he chatted. He seemed in no rush to help me at all, which was disappointing because Georgia seemed so certain that Jim would give me a place to stay. She'd made it very, very clear that he "owed" her. I didn't really know what that meant. All I knew was that something had happened between the two of them long ago and now she was calling in a favor.

For me.

To be honest, I thought she had called him already. Otherwise, I wouldn't have had the guts to do what I was doing: showing up in a stranger's bar. Although this space was a really cozy, dim sort of bar. It was the kind of place I probably would have spent time in during my early 20s.

Now, at just past the ripe old age of 30, I wasn't so sure that this was the place I'd be hanging out. Even in this space, with the single entrance and the cozy atmosphere, I felt too scared. Too isolated. Too constricted.

I needed my freedom.

That was my plan: to find freedom. I didn't exactly have all of the details worked out. Step one was just to find a place where I could rest for a little while. Dwayne and Mike had hunted me for a little while. I didn't realize there had been a tracker in the car I'd stolen from them, so the first day I'd run away had been a nightmare. They seemed to be constantly right on my ass, but then I'd finally gotten smart and I'd ditched the car.

Using the money I'd swiped from Dwayne's office the day I'd run away, I got a shitty used car that had somehow – and I didn't really know how – gotten me to Rawr County.

And now I was in a bar.

And I felt like the walls were closing in a little bit.

Glancing around, I started to sweat. There had to be another exit. Right? Back in the area that was labeled EMPLOYEES ONLY. There had to be an extra door. It would be a fire hazard not to.

Wouldn't it?

I took a deep breath as I looked around. I couldn't seem to stop moving.

Everything's going to be fine. Calm down. You have to calm the fuck down.

That was an easy thing to tell myself. It was a much harder thing to actually do.

"Listen, I've got a visitor here at the bar. Young lady. Goes by the name of," he glanced over at me and raised an eyebrow. That was my cue.

"Darla," I sighed. If he actually was talking to Georgia, then it didn't matter. He'd let her know exactly who I was and what I wanted.

"Darla," he repeated. "You know her? Ah."

I waited.

He waited.

The two of us stood there. He was listening, though. I wasn't sure what I was supposed to be doing, so I started fidgeting. Maybe if I was careful enough, stood still enough, he'd forget I was here and I could quietly sneak back out the door without any problems. I knew it was too late for that, though. I kissed "easy" goodbye a long time ago.

Getting yourself caught by an evil magician and his best friend will do that to a girl.

The man kept nodding and eventually, he made a non-committal nod. He bid her farewell, and then he hung up the phone.

"So," he said, turning back to me. His slightly villainous persona was gone. The anger and irritation had melted away and had been replaced with something else: something I didn't want to see.

Pity.

Wasn't that great?

I'd hoped that I could come here and find a way to blend in. I didn't need this stranger to feel *sorry* for me. Not beyond wanting to do a good deed and letting me hide out for a little while.

I sighed. "You talked to Georgia."

"I did."

"Did she tell you I need a place to stay? Did she already tell you that?" I started wringing my hands anxiously. I couldn't go back out in the world alone. Even if this guy, Jim, was going to be irritable with me, I needed him to let me stay.

Just for a little while.

Just for a bit.

Georgia didn't work at the diner I'd wandered into on a regular basis. She was only there to cover a shift for a friend, which meant it was even stranger that I'd managed to be there on the one night she was hanging out serving food.

To me, this meant that my journey to Wishville was fate.

It had to be.

Rawr County was a big place. Even if I'd known this was a shifter area, it didn't mean much if I couldn't find a safe place to hide out. That was what I really needed right now. I needed a place to blend in until I figured out what to do next.

I didn't know if I needed to prosecute the man who stole me or if I needed to just figure out how to get the guts to kill him.

Either way, I knew that eventually, he was going to come for me.

I didn't want to give him a heads-up as to where I was. Not before I was ready. Not before I had a plan of how I was going to stay safe.

"No," he said slowly.

"That's impossible. She told me she called Jim."

"That might be true."

"So, what's the deal?" I was starting to get even more anxious. I crossed my arms over my chest and wished I'd chosen to wear something other than the thin tank top I'd slipped on that morning. My jeans kept my legs warm, but the tank top did nothing to warm the chill that was currently shooting through my body.

Maybe this place wasn't usually very cold, but right now, the guy in here was giving me the iciest stare I'd ever gotten.

It was only three in the afternoon, so it wasn't like he was opening the bar for patrons anytime soon. Georgia had been very clear on that. I was supposed to arrive early enough in the day that nobody was going to be here but him.

That was it.

I was supposed to drive my crappy little Honda up here, park it in the parking lot while avoiding all of the potholes, and then march inside and ask for Jim.

That was it.

Only, something was wrong.

When the man opened his mouth and spoke, my heart fell.

"I'm not Jim."

2

Kapono

She was in trouble.

I could smell it on her the moment she walked into the bar. The scent of fear wafted from this woman, along with something like lavender body wash and vanilla shampoo.

She was enticing.

"You're not Jim?"

When she spoke, I could hear her voice crack. My heart almost shattered at the sound because it wasn't me that she wanted. It was my business partner, Jim. The two of us had opened this bar years ago because we both loved drinking and we both wanted a safe, comfortable place for the younger shifters of Rawr County to be able to go.

"I'm not Jim," I told her.

"Did I come to the wrong bar?"

"No."

Her eyes narrowed. There we go. That was the fire I wanted to see. I didn't want to look at this woman and think about her being weak or scared or timid. I wanted to see the fire. The passion. I wanted to see the strength within her eyes as she looked forward to her future.

"Then could you please tell me where the fuck I can find Jim?"

"No."

Glaring, she turned and started marching back toward the front door. Being something of a pretentious prick, I waited until her hand was on the knob to call out to her.

"I don't know where he is."

She paused. Turned around. Raised an eyebrow.

"You don't know?"

"I don't know. He was supposed to be here today, but I got a text from him about an hour ago that said he couldn't make it. He asked me to cover him. Guess now I know why."

"I'm supposed to stay with him," she told me.

"You?"

"Yes."

"With Jim?"

"Is that so hard to believe?"

"Yes."

"Why?"

"Because Jim doesn't exactly have time for women."

That silenced her. Georgia hadn't told me anything of note about this woman - only that she was a friend who needed a place to stay. Since Jim wasn't around today, Georgia asked me to take care of her. I wasn't very close friends with Georgia. I knew her only because she and her husband were buddies with Jim and his husband. We'd all hung out a couple of times over the years, but nothing I would call serious. Georgia was the kind of person I'd chit-chat with for about ten minutes at a party. She wasn't someone I would send a friend in trouble to.

"Do you know when he's going to be back?"

"I don't."

"Shit."

The woman looked around the room, biting her lip as she took in her surroundings.

Darla.

She'd said her name was Darla.

It was a pretty name: one of the best I'd heard. I'd love to whisper it to her. I'd love to slide my tongue down her cheek as I murmured her name in her ear.

I bet she'd like it, too.

And I bet she was good in bed. She was fiery and gorgeous as hell. I didn't much care for the fact that she was obviously scared of something, but I'd love to throw her down on my bed and spend hours just exploring her many curves.

I'd make her forget.

Whatever the hell was bothering her, I'd make it stop.

I'd get rid of it.

She was afraid of something happening, afraid of something bothering her or catching her, and I hated that.

If she was my girl, I wouldn't let her be scared.

I'd protect her.

I looked at her now and really took in everything about her. She had long hair and soft skin, and her curves were not the least bit hidden under her tiny tank top and jeans. I loved it. I'd do just about anything to get my hands on that ass of hers. I'd grab her and pull her up against me, and then I'd just *kiss* her.

I wasn't the kind of man who wanted to date someone who was stick-thin. Not that there was anything wrong with someone who was slender. I just personally preferred when a woman had a little bit of meat on her bones, and Darla did. She was thick. Pretty. She was the kind of woman who looked so wildly sexy that I bet she didn't even know what she was doing to my dick right then.

I cleared my throat and tried to clear my head.

"What do you need?"

"Excuse me?"

"What do you need? From Jim?"

"I'm supposed to stay with him," she said slowly. She took a step back from the counter and walked over to the nearest high top. She ran her fingers over it before turning back to me. "I'm supposed to have a place to be safe." I was still standing behind the bar, cell phone in hand. I set it down on the bar and just stared at the gorgeous creature in front of me. My hands were flat on the bar, and I cocked my head, looking at her.

"Georgia said you needed help."

She nodded. "I do." She clasped her hands together and looked down at them. "I do."

Those two little words were going to be my undoing. I didn't consider myself to be a particularly nice person, but I also didn't do things like turn away women who needed help.

Right now, she needed me, and I wondered if she was going to say anything else. When she didn't speak, I shrugged. I was trying to seem as casual as I could, but the reality was that I felt anything but. On the inside, my entire body felt like it was on fire.

I wanted to save her.

Keep her.

Protect her.

I could do that.

Jim had missed his chance at protecting this lady. Besides, Jim had a husband: Kellan. The two of them were very happily married and had been for some time. They didn't need to protect this woman.

I did.

I'd protect her.

My inner-tiger wanted to come out and play with hers. I could tell right away that the two of us were the same. We were both tigers, but more than that, we were both loners.

And oh, I wanted to save her.

I had friends in Rawr County. Perhaps I didn't have as many as I should have, but still, I had connections. I had people who would protect me and keep me safe and sane.

She didn't.

She didn't have anyone.

"I can help you the best I can, but you need to be straight with me," I warned her.

"Straight with you?" Darla shook her head just the slightest bit, as though she didn't understand what I was saying.

"You need to tell me what the deal is because if you don't, I can't help you. Wishville is a small town. It doesn't seem like it, but all of Rawr County has that small town vibe. People here know each other. They look out for each other. Even if you wander into some of the other areas throughout the county, you're going to find that most of us are familiar with the big shifter names."

When people realized there was someone new hanging around the bar, they were going to notice. Georgia had done right by sending this woman to Jim, but I was going to be the one to protect her. I needed it. Right now, more than any other time at all, I wanted to protect her.

She cocked her head and took a step forward. Placing her fingers on the edge of the bar, she started tapping them. It looked like she was playing the piano.

What song was running through her head?

What was she thinking?

"So, what are you saying?"

"I'm saying you need to tell me whatever it is that you're going through right now."

She took a deep breath. For just a moment, I thought she was going to lie to me. Either that or run out the door. She didn't, though. Instead, she nodded, and when she spoke, it was the truth.

"I'm running away."

She was being honest.

"Good girl," I nodded, approving of what she'd said. I didn't like that she was running. I didn't like that she'd been put into the position where she *had* to run, but she'd been bold to say what the truth was.

She stared at me. Her jaw dropped just a little.

"What did you call me?"

"I called you a good girl."

"Why?"

I reached across the counter and grabbed her chin. My grip was firm, but not painful. She was probably getting a little tired of me just leaning across the bar and touching her like I owned the place, but I did, in fact, own the place.

"Because you're doing a good job, pretty tiger."

"H-H-How did you know I was a tiger?"

"Because I'm one, too."

3

Darla

I stared at the man.

"You can't be."

He laughed. "I'm a lot of things, Darla, but I'm not a liar. I would appreciate it if you don't call me one again."

"Of course," I shook my head. "I'm really sorry."

That was the moment I realized I didn't actually know his name. He seemed to realize it at the same time because he grinned.

"Kapono."

"That's an interesting name."

"Thank you."

"Hawaiian?"

He nodded. "I was born and raised there. I moved to Colorado for college and promptly dropped out. Met Jim. The two of us became buddies and the rest is history."

"What was your major?"

He looked at me curiously. "Nobody ever asks me that."

I shrugged. "Call me curious, I suppose."

"It was art."

"An art major?"

"Yep."

"And you dropped out?"

"Yeah, as it turns out, I like looking at art a lot more than I like producing it."

"Seems like you've done all right," I gestured to the space around us. The bar was a cool place. A bit of a dive, but still. I wasn't the kind of person who was going to complain about any of that. I'd never considered myself to be fancy, and despite the fact that I was something of a total weirdo, I didn't feel any need to change who I was.

At least, I didn't feel the need to change into anyone fancier than who I was.

"Thank you," he smiled. "If you notice the original artwork on any of the walls, that was mostly done by me."

I'd seen it.

There were drawings and paintings of bears and tigers, lions and zebras. I'd even noticed a couple of red pandas and one particularly lovely drawing of a tiny goose. They were pretty. This place made being a shapeshifter seem not quite so terrible.

"It looks like you're a better artist than you've given yourself credit for," I pointed out.

"I give myself plenty of credit," he laughed. "Just ask Jim."

Speaking of Jim...

I looked up at Kapono. He was handsome, all right. He was probably married, too, although a quick glance at his hand revealed he didn't wear a ring. That wasn't unusual for shapeshifters, at least according to the brief conversation I'd had with Georgia. Most of them didn't wear a lot of jewelry. You kind of just had to know who was married and who wasn't.

Not that I'd known a lot of shapeshifters.

Not that I'd known *any*.

"So," I said, "can I stay here until he gets back?"

It almost felt like asking too much. I knew that this guy, Kapono, was probably busy. The bar was going to open in a little while and he'd probably have his hands full taking care of customers and keeping things running smoothly.

Still, I didn't really want to go sit and wait in my car until Jim came back.

What if he wasn't coming in at all today?

I was out of money. I had enough to fill the gas tank one more time plus a meal or two, but that was it. If anything else went wrong – like I had to get a hotel – then I'd be totally screwed. I was hungry, and I was tired, and I just wanted a place where I could rest my head for a couple of days.

Kapono watched me for a moment with a calculated sort of gaze. I still couldn't get a real, honest read on him, but he kind of made my heart flutter. I wasn't sure what *that* was all about. He made me feel like I was okay. No, he made me feel better than okay. He made me feel *sexy*.

I wasn't sure if it was the throat-grabbing or the chin-grabbing that had done it for me, really, but I liked the fact that he was hot as hell and not afraid to invade my space a little bit. He seemed kind of bossy and a little bit demanding, but even that might not have been a bad thing. Not entirely.

"Stay here?"

"At the restaurant."

He considered this for a moment.

"I don't know when Jim's coming back. Could be tonight. Could be tomorrow."

I nodded, swallowing hard. I couldn't tell if this was a rejection or not. I also didn't know where I was going to go.

Then, before I had to panic, Kapono spoke again. His deep, rumbly voice held promise and comfort, and I found myself clinging to every word.

"We open soon. Can you wait tables?"

I nodded. I could pretty much do anything. Back when I'd been the star of a magic show, I'd had to do a lot of different things. One of them was waiting tables when I wasn't on stage. I'd never really wanted a life where I was considered famous or got crazy attention from people, so my job had been painful and uncomfortable for me.

And calling it a "job" was simply a lie.

It was a way of thinking I utilized in order to feel safe. If I thought "I had a job," it kept me from realizing, "I was a prisoner."

If I thought of myself as simply having a working condition in which I was miserable, it was a way that I could feel like everything would be okay eventually.

Someday.

"Good."

"Aren't you going to ask what I'm running from?" I asked him, confused and surprised that he hadn't wanted more details. He knew I was in trouble. Right now he was just talking about waiting tables.

"Do you think it's something that concerns me?"

"Not really."

"Do you think I need to know?"

I shook my head.

"Then you don't have to tell me. We do, however, need a cover story for you."

"A cover story?" I swallowed and licked my lips. My mouth felt dry all of a sudden. When was the last time I'd actually had a drink? Kapono seemed to realize this because he reached for a glass, filled it with ice water, and handed it to me. I chugged it and he refilled the glass. That time, I sipped at it slowly lest I seem like the kind of person who didn't take care of herself.

"You can't just waltz into my bar and start waiting tables."

"Why not?"

Kapono laughed. He actually laughed. I felt a little silly. To me, it didn't make a lot of sense as to why I couldn't just start working.

Surely bars hired people all of the time.

Kapono's bar, it seemed, was different. Maybe Jim didn't like hiring new people. Perhaps the two of them had some sort of agreement as to how hiring went.

He just shook his head. He seemed to do that a lot around me.

"Because Sloan, the pride and joy of this bar, isn't the kind of bartender who is going to randomly hire a new waitress without telling the entire customer base that I'm hiring. If you're going to start work tonight, we need a damn good reason."

So, it was a tight knit little group. That was something I could understand. I understood it and maybe I could find a way to work within the limitations that presented.

"You could say I'm your cousin," I offered.

"Darling, I appreciate that, but nobody will buy it."

"Why not?"

"We look nothing alike."

"We're both tigers, though." That had to count for something.

"Trust me, honey, if I had an adopted cousin who was as gorgeous as you, everyone in town would know about it."

I stared at him, blinking. Was this for real? Was he really saying that he thought I was pretty?

"Don't look so surprised."

"I am surprised."

"Why? Has nobody ever told you that you're gorgeous before?"

I shook my head.

No.

No, words like "gorgeous" were not things anyone had ever uttered to me.

It had been quite the opposite, in fact. People had told me I was a freak. Damaged. Broken. That was the reason I hadn't tried to escape before. I'd been told so many times that nobody would ever want me and eventually, I started to believe it.

"No."

"Are you fucking kidding me?"

There it was.

The deep, terrifying voice of a man who was angry.

And I didn't know what to do.

I didn't know how to react to this enormous man who seemed so very irritated at the way someone had treated me.

I *knew* that he wasn't mad at me.

I understood, logically, that I wasn't the person he had a problem with.

What I didn't understand was how his voice still managed to be so scary.

What I didn't get was how this dude was so intimidating.

This guy was *terrifying*. Kapono was big. He towered over me, and I was no dainty woman, so that was really saying something.

"I'm not...kidding you."

Only, I could tell that his anger wasn't directed at me. His anger was directed at whoever had hurt me. Whoever had been cruel to me. I kind of liked that feeling.

It was like Kapono was on my side.

He wasn't my friend. Not really, but he was on my side.

"Those people are fucking idiots," he said.

"Um, thank you. I guess."

A sense of satisfaction filled me at the realization that suddenly, I had someone on my side.

"You're welcome. You're fucking lovely," he said.

And then, my eyes widened. At that moment, I scented something in the air, something very sweet. It was something I hadn't expected to smell ever. Not like this.

Arousal.

Excitement.

Delight.

When I'd been part of the magic show, I'd been overwhelmed with smells. People had come in to see the freak who could shift into a tiger and back again as a naked lady over and over. They'd been thrilled.

Kapono wasn't making me feel the way they did, though. He wasn't leering at me. He didn't seem to think I was some sort of worthless woman who was only good for sex. He didn't make me feel cheap the way that other people had.

No, when Kapono looked at me, it felt good.

And when he looked at me, I started thinking that maybe I might actually want him to want to have sex with me. I knew it would probably make me a freak, but I didn't really care. I was starting to feel like maybe, everything was going to be okay.

Like maybe, I was going to be safe.

"Say you're my bride," he said suddenly.

"What?"

I must have misheard him.

"My bride," he said.

Okay, so I hadn't misheard.

"Like, your wife?"

He nodded. "Why not?"

"Um, because we don't know anything about each other, and also...wouldn't people know if you were going to get married?"

"Maybe," he shrugged.

"Maybe?"

"Look, I kind of have a reputation as being difficult to get to know. Some have even called me emotionally unavailable."

It was his turn to drum his fingers on the counter as he looked at me. He wiggled his eyebrows. He was excited by this.

"That's not really something you should be bragging about," I pointed out. Emotionally unavailable? Really?

"Oh, I'm not bragging. I'm just sharing."

"Why?" Also, someone who was "emotionally unavailable" probably wouldn't be sharing their deep, dark secrets.

Right?

"Because I want you to know that nobody in their right mind will ever question this. They'll be relieved."

"What?"

I couldn't do that. I just wanted a place to stay, to lie low for a couple of days. I didn't really need a boyfriend or a husband.

"I don't think this is a good idea," I told him.

"It's the perfect cover."

"Are you serious?"

"Yes. Trust me."

And for some reason, I did. For some reason, I trusted him completely. I couldn't explain why. I couldn't figure out what it was about Kapono that just let me know he wasn't going to hurt me.

I didn't have much time to think about it, though, because the door to the bar burst open and a slender blonde woman marched in. She was wearing a corset top with tight leather pants and boots that had to be like five or six inches high.

"Good, you're here," she said to Kapono as she marched right by me and slid behind the counter. "Did Jim already talk to you about what happened last night?"

"Not yet." Kapono winked at me, as if to say just be patient. I knew that whatever was happening next, it was going to be okay. He wasn't asking me to sit around all night, but he was going to handle whatever this thing was.

"Shit. Well, there was a bit of a fight."

"A fight?" Instantly, his demeanor changed.

"Yeah. Tony and Bagel were in here."

"Bagel?" I asked before I could stop myself.

"Bagel is known for making the best bagels in town," Kapono told me. I'd interrupted, though, and I'd alerted the lady that I was here. Suddenly, she looked me up and down as she tried to figure out who I was and why I was in *her* bar. Even though I knew it was Kapono's place, I wondered if she was the woman he'd mentioned earlier. The bartender. If she was, then it sounded like not very much would get by her.

"Who are you?"

I stared at the woman. She glared at me, and I got the distinct impression that she didn't like me. I had no idea why considering the fact that I'd just gotten here.

I wasn't sure what to say, but fortunately, Kapono answered for me.

"This is my wife," he lied easily. He stepped out from behind the bar, walked around to my slide, and slipped his arm around me. I was still standing, and now that he was right next to me, it was easy to see just how much bigger he was than me.

I kind of liked it.

I felt safe with him. He was strong and big and, well, durable.

And he'd just announced that I was his wife.

Well.

We had no details worked out. We didn't have a plan. We had nothing. All we had was a shared understanding that I needed help and he was offering me that help even if it was in a way that was somewhat...unconventional.

"What the hell?"

"Yep," he nodded.

"Are you fucking with me?"

"No," I shook my head. "I'm Darla. Nice to meet you."

The woman ignored me and stared at Kapono. Her eyes widened. She glanced at our bare hands which definitely did *not* have wedding rings and then looked back at his face.

"You're married?"

"I'm married," Kapono said. He almost sounded proud, and despite the fact that this was a fake marriage, it made me feel pretty good that he was happy with this. I wasn't so new to the world that I didn't realize what was actually going on. Kapono most likely had an ulterior motive of some kind that I didn't know about.

"To Darla?"

The woman pointed to me, as though there was anyone else in the bar that Kapono could possibly have claimed he was married to.

He chuckled. "To Darla."

She gawked. "When were you going to tell everyone?"

"We wanted to keep it quiet," I interrupted, deciding suddenly to try to take charge a little. My interruption got her attention, and she turned back to me.

"Keep it quiet?"

Kapono was a quick thinker. I had to give him credit for that.

"Sloan, Darla's family can be a bit intense."

"Yeah," I nodded, quickly figuring out what to say. It was like once I started lying, it just got easier and easier. "Intense is a nice word. A more accurate representation would be saying that if you think Tony and Bagel are bad, wait until you meet my brothers."

THE TIGER'S PRETEND HUSBAND

"Say no more," Sloan held up a hand. "My brothers are total dicks." Her face furrowed into a little frown, as though just the thought of her brothers caused her anxiety. I felt a little bad for making up a fake dysfunctional family, but she was going along with it.

"Really?"

"You have no clue. Growing up the youngest kid in a family of eight with the rest all being boys was a nightmare." Sloan shuddered. I didn't blame her. Having seven older brothers couldn't have been easy no matter how you sliced it.

"Ah, it wasn't all bad, Sloan," Kapono winked at her. "Your brothers were always there to check in on you before you went on dates."

She glared. "They were there to screen my dates. It was a service I didn't ask for, by the way." She shook her head and turned back to me. "Anyway, no clue why Kapono kept you a secret, but he's a weirdo. Congrats on the wedding. Nice to meet you."

And that was it.

She believed him.

Why the hell did she believe him?

I glanced over at Kapono. He caught my eye and grinned, as if to say, "see?"

He'd done it.

He'd successfully tricked someone into believing that the two of us had *something*. He'd gotten her to believe that we were married and it had taken exactly zero effort for either of us.

I wanted to ask him what his secret was. Maybe Kapono was just so wildly unpredictable that nobody really thought twice about his decisions because when it came to the tiger bartender, he always made the least expected decision.

And now I was going to be playing the role of his wife.

Looking back at the beautiful blonde lady who was standing behind the bar, I decided it was time to keep talking. I had to establish that I wasn't scared. I wasn't afraid. That was what I *needed* people to believe about me.

It wasn't true, of course. None of it was. I was totally, completely petrified of just about everything, but at the end of the day, I was going to be okay.

At the end of the day, me and Kapono were getting away with this decision, and I was going to be safe.

I was going to *find* safety.

No matter what the cost was.

"I'm going to be working tonight," I piped up. Again, I wasn't sure where this raw energy was coming from. Normally, I tried to shrink into a tiny ball and become as small as I possibly could, but today I felt different. Today it was like everything was different somehow, and I just wanted to get out of that shell.

I'd been locked in a cage for so damn long that breaking free felt like magic.

I wanted to harness that.

"Working?"

"I told her she could waitress," Kapono said. "You cool with that?"

Sloan looked me up and down. "You good at dealing with 21-year-old pricks?"

"I once single-handedly served alcohol to my ex-boyfriend's entire frat house on a dare and not only did I not spill any drinks, I didn't punch anyone, either."

"Impressive. You good thinking on your feet?"

"I've been known to hold my own."

"Yeah, okay," she shrugged. "I'm pretty new, but I feel like I'm doing a good job as the resident bartender these days. I've only been here a few weeks and so far, I've gotten my ass handed to me on more than one occasion. It'll be nice to have some more girl power around here."

"Can't wait," I smiled. I glanced over at Kapono, and he gave me a little nod.

I couldn't wait at all.

4

Kapono

Shortly after midnight, Jim called. I stepped into the employee break room and answered the phone. Irritation, shock, and surprise all washed over me. He should have warned me. He should have told me.

Also, he shouldn't have bailed on me today.

He still hadn't let me know where he was. He'd only said that he wasn't going to make it into work today and that I needed to hold down the fort for him.

Well, "holding down the fort" had somehow ended up with me being fake-married to the hottest damn woman I'd seen *ever*.

Raising the phone to my ear, I snapped at him.

"What the hell?"

A pause.

Then, "What do you mean?"

"What the hell? That's what I mean. What the fuck, man?" I ran a hand through my hair. I'd just announced to the damn world that Darla was my wife and I had no idea why I'd fucking done it. It was like I couldn't control myself around her. My animal side, the more rambunctious and wild side of myself, seemed to think that it was a good idea.

Well, it wasn't.

None of it was.

I was supposed to be hiding her, keeping her locked away. I didn't know what she was running from. Georgia had been very,

very vague and when I'd tried calling her back later, she'd sent my call to voicemail. Of course.

"Oh," Jim suddenly seemed to realize what was going on. "You mean Darla."

"Yes, I mean Darla. You might have told me there's a woman in danger you're supposed to be guarding."

"Look, I meant to. I really did. I got called away, though, and I panicked. I honestly completely forgot."

I softened my voice. "Your mom?"

"Yeah," he whispered.

"She okay?"

"No."

"What's going on, friend?"

Jim's mom was sick. Shifters weren't supposed to get sick the way that humans did, but sometimes being a shifter didn't really matter as much as we all wanted it to. Sometimes shifters got injured just the same way that humans did, and sometimes that meant we had to say goodbye earlier than we wanted to.

"Doctors gave her a week. Maybe two."

"You wanna stay with her?"

"You don't mind?"

"Not at all."

"Is Kellan with you?"

"Yeah."

"Good."

Jim's husband, Kellan, had been a rock during this time. Kellan and Jim had been an item for as long as I could remember, which meant that Jim's mom was just as much Kellan's mother as Jim's. The three of them loved spending time together baking. They were always trying to give Bagel a run for his money. Jim and Kellan would bring their goods to the bar on the same nights that Bagel would and every customer would get a free snack.

"Stay as long as you need," I told Jim. I could handle things at One More Howl on my own for a little while. We had a good team. I could ask Sloan to work a little more and there was no way she'd say no. She was saving up and would love having additional hours.

"You mean it?" Jim's voice was a mixture of relieved and still unbelieving.

"I mean it."

"You sure you can handle the bar without me?"

"I've handled it plenty of times without you," I reminded him. The two of us worked together like a well-oiled machine. Jim and I could do pretty much everything we needed together.

"This is different."

"How is it different?"

"You've got an extra person there now. How is she, by the way?"

"Darla?"

"Yeah."

"Scared. You feel like filling me in on that?"

"You called Georgia?"

"I did."

"Then you know as much as me. Seems she showed up in the diner one night. Georgia was working to cover a shift for Savannah. Saw her. Knew she had to help. You know how tigers are."

"Yeah." I knew how tigers were. I was one, too, after all.

"Where you going to put her? You can hide her at our place."

"Actually," I rubbed my temples. I wasn't sure whether I should be telling him or not. "I actually said she could work here."

Silence.

"I don't know if that's a good idea. We just hired Sloan recently and there's a waiting list of people who want waitressing positions. Everyone will freak out that we didn't go in order."

"I'm aware."

"Then why would you say she could work there? How are you explaining it away?"

Shit.

I hadn't planned on admitting this out loud just now, but he was going to find out soon anyway. It was going to be better for all of us if Jim heard this from me.

"Oh, I told everyone we're married."

Silence.

Then Jim made a sound I hadn't heard him make in a very long time.

Jim laughed.

*

That night, when we closed up, we split the tips, wiped down the tables and counters, swept, mopped, and finished doing the dishes. Then Sloan left, along with our bouncer of the evening. We didn't always have one, but I'd been trying to make sure there was someone who could at least walk people back to their cars if they got scared or worried.

"So," Darla said, looking at me. She held out the wad of cash I'd given to her. "You can take this. I know you probably had to give it to me in front of Sloan so it looked normal and stuff, but I don't need it."

I stared at her. "Honey, you probably need it more than any of us. In fact, here." I handed her my share of the tips and she looked at the money like it was poison.

"I can't take it."

"Then just save it. You should take it, though."

The look of utter relief on Darla's face told me it had been the right decision, and she shoved the money in her back jeans pocket.

"Thanks."

I nodded. "Time for us to go home."

"Home?"

"To my place," I said.

"Are you sure you don't mind?"

"You want to tell me what you're running from?" I asked, crossing my arms over my chest.

"Not yet."

"Then yeah, let's get back to my place. I want to know you're safe."

"I drove myself here," she said. "I could follow you."

I watched her for a minute and considered this. It was dark out, though, and while I didn't live very far, I didn't want to take the chance that Darla might accidentally get separated from me in the darkness.

"I'll ride with you," I told her. "You can bring me back tomorrow to get my car."

"Are...are you sure?"

"I'd offer to drive us, but I'm guessing you'd like to have your own way to escape if you need to, right?"

She nodded, and the scent of relief filled the air of the empty bar.

She felt safe.

*

When we got back to the house nearly twenty minutes later, I was thrilled to be home.

"Finally," I said, collapsing on the couch. Darla said nothing. Instead, she stood in the middle of the doorway and looked around. The most interesting thing about her was how she tried to take in everything all at once. I got the feeling that not very much got by Darla. She was constantly watching everything. Her eyes roamed from the flower-printed couches to the thrift store art to the collection of mismatched throw rugs I had on the ground.

"What is it?" I asked her. I wanted to know what she was thinking. When she looked at this space, what did she think? What did she see? Did she look at this place and see the potential? Did she look at it and see a nightmare? I had no real way of knowing except for the fact that she didn't know how to control her emotions yet. Her scents were going crazy. Darla smelled like excitement and happiness and peace.

How long had it been since she had felt any of those things? That was probably a better question.

"It's just not really what I expected." She crossed her arms over her chest and leaned against the doorway. My house wasn't anything fancy, but I liked it. A lot of shifters liked to go big and fancy with their houses, but not me. In my opinion, a big house just meant more to clean. I wanted to spend my time outside. I didn't want to spend it hanging out mopping.

"What's not really what you expected?"

"Your place."

"What did you expect?"

"I guess what I expected was that you'd have an apartment. You know, maybe above the bar." Darla gestured around, as though I didn't realize what she was talking about.

"What do you mean?" I'd never considered living above the bar before. To be honest, it wasn't something I was sure I would like. I'd bought my house a long time ago. It was located on the edge of Rawr County, which meant I was close to everything I needed to be close to. There was nothing but empty space between me and the next county, so I had all of the freedom in the world.

If I wanted to go run, I could.

If I wanted to go hunt, I could.

If I wanted to throw myself at the sexiest tiger shifter in town whom I may have told everyone I was married to, I could.

"What's wrong with this place?"

"Nothing. It just doesn't really suit you."

"And what would suit me?"

"I seriously picture you in a place with exposed brick. You have that kind of vibe."

I laughed and shook my head. Then, leaning back against the couch, I kicked off my shoes one at a time.

"You can come inside," I told her. She was still standing in the doorway, still not sure whether she was going to come in or stay out. "I don't bite." That was a lie.

I'd bite her.

Out of every girl in the entire county, I would bite her more than anyone. I wanted to dig my teeth into her soft flesh and just nibble.

Darla was the best.

"I know," she told me.

"Just not ready?"

"No."

"That's okay," I shrugged. "You can take your time."

She could take all of the time she needed, but I wasn't going to sit here and watch her stand in the doorway. It was the end of a long night. In a few hours, morning would be here. I wanted to get in a good run before that happened. I wasn't much of an "up with the birds" kind of guy. Instead, I liked running just before the sun came up and then going to bed and sleeping the day away.

"What are you doing?" Darla suddenly seemed to notice I was slipping my shirt off. I wasn't embarrassed by my body. Yes, I was pretty fit. Most shifters were. Still, that didn't really mean anything when it came to issues of self-esteem. Just because someone was fit or not fit didn't mean they were comfortable with their body or uncomfortable with it.

"I'm taking my shirt off," I told her like it was the simplest thing in the world.

"Why?"

"What's with all the questions? Aren't you tired?"

"No," she said.

"Then come inside, Darla. Close the door."

5

Darla

This didn't seem real. None of it seemed real. I was actually standing in the house of a handsome tiger shifter, and he was giving me a place to stay for the night.

When I'd taken Georgia up on her offer to find Jim, I hadn't really expected that Jim wouldn't be around or that I'd end up staying with his friend.

In fact, the only thing I really had expected was that I'd get a small reprieve from trying to run.

That was what I was really tired of. I was tired of running. Now, for the first time, I finally felt like I was going to get a chance to be free. I was going to get a chance to breathe.

Unfortunately for me, Kapono wasn't the kind of guy who was chill or calm, and he certainly didn't seem like he was the kind of guy who was going to allow me some restful peace.

No, he was going to keep me on the edge of my seat until he saved my heart or broke it.

I didn't know which one it was going to be.

Kapono was the kind of guy who was so damn handsome he took my breath away.

These were feelings that I wasn't used to. I wasn't used to being around someone who took my *breath* away, someone who made my heart stop.

I kind of hated it.

And I kind of loved it.

"Do you want to go run?"

His question broke through my thoughts. I stared at him, blinking.

"Run?"

"You know, like shifters do," he smiled. His eyes twinkled as he looked at me. Running wasn't something I did often, or at all. When I shifted, it was always on demand. It was always because I was being forced to do it.

Now it sounded like I was being given a chance for the very first time, and I didn't know if I was supposed to or not.

Running?

Was that something shifters really liked to do?

Was it actually a bad idea?

Or would it be a little bit fun?

Maybe running with Kapono could be relaxing or calming. Maybe it was just the motivation I needed to keep going. It had been a long night. It had been fun, sure, but it had been long, and I was tired.

"I don't know," I finally said.

"No?"

"No."

"You don't know if you want to run?"

I shook my head.

I didn't.

Why didn't I know?

And why couldn't I decide?

It was the first time I'd been faced with the actual option of choosing, and I just...wasn't sure.

"I don't know if I want to run." My voice sounded small and weak. Tiny.

"Do you want a minute to think about it?" Kapono asked, stretching. "Or do you want me to convince you?"

When he said it like that, I thought I was going to absolutely melt. I couldn't really believe that Kapono was saying this to me. It wasn't like he was saying anything bad. He wasn't.

It was more like, I wasn't used to someone showing me affection. I wasn't used to someone showing me any sort of interest.

And I liked this.

I liked the intrigue.

But maybe I wasn't reading into the situation correctly. Perhaps he wasn't really saying what I thought he was saying. Maybe he was...

Well, maybe it wasn't quite right.

I needed to be sure.

"Convince me?"

He nodded.

"How would you convince me?"

Oh, this was a dangerous game we were playing. Everyone in town suddenly thought we were married, which meant everyone was going to expect us to be physically affectionate with each other. Still, I hadn't really planned on starting with the PDA just yet. I'd planned on taking my time, figuring out what I was going to do next, and moving on from there.

"I have quite a few ways."

"Do you have tricks?" I licked my lips. I didn't mean to. It was just that Kapono was...

Well, he was a lot of fun.

He was fun, and for the first time in what seemed like a million years, I wasn't hanging out worried that I was going to be attacked or forced back into a cage. I wasn't waiting for someone to hurt me.

I was just...

I was just being.

"I have some tricks."

"Like what?"

"I could show you, if you like."

He was asking my permission, which was sweet. It was also something I wasn't really used to. In the past, people had just taken what they wanted from me. They hadn't actually asked whether I would give them permission or not.

I should have said no.

I knew that I was supposed to say no. You weren't supposed to let strange men offer to "convince" you of things, especially when those things probably involved sex.

That was what Kapono reminded me of.

Sex.

He wasn't the kind of guy who had neat, tidy sex. He didn't keep it simple and he definitely didn't do missionary position.

No way.

Kapono was the kind of man who fucked. I knew without any sort of logical explanation or reasoning that he was the kind of person who took a woman to bed and took her to bed. When he made love to someone, they were going to be a sweaty, gooey mess by the time everything was over and they were done.

I just knew it.

"I want you to convince me to go run with you," I said.

He smirked, and then he stood up from his place on the couch. His shirt was off. He'd taken it off a few minutes ago and tossed it to the side, but now that he was standing, his abs looked even better. I felt like "rippling" was an apt way to describe them. Yes, Kapono seemed to have rippling abs. He walked across the living room and made his way toward me without hesitating.

There was no hesitation.

No pausing.

No second guessing.

I stood where I was in the doorway and hoped my heart wasn't beating out of my chest. He was like me, I knew. A shapeshifter. I didn't know much about shapeshifters, to be honest, but I knew that the two of us were the same. We had this in common, and we were alike.

More than that, we were both cats.

He looked like a cat now. He looked like he was prowling across the carpets as he made his way to me. When he reached the doorway, he placed his hands above me and gripped the doorframe. I worried he was going to break it.

"Look at me," he said, and when I did, he kissed me.

This was no gentle kiss.

No dainty, well-mannered kiss.

Nope.

It was dirty.

Messy.

Feral.

He was feral.

He claimed my mouth like he was in charge of me. He kissed me like he was hungry for me, like he needed me. In that moment, I felt possessed by him. I felt utterly and totally weak when facing him.

When he pulled away, I was breathless. A smirk slid across his face.

"Have I convinced you yet?"

I shook my head. I couldn't give in that easy. I had to be stronger than that. I had to be better than that.

"No."

"No?" Kapono raised an eyebrow. "Really?"

"Really," I whispered. My entire body felt like it was on fire, though. I was breathing hard already, which was kind of embarrassing, but I didn't want to give him the satisfaction of taking me too easily.

He wanted to convince me that I should go running with him, right?

Well, I'd let him convince me.

"You're a tough girl," he told me.

"I'm a tiger." I wasn't really a girl at all. Not really. I'd learned long ago that being a tiger was the first thing people realized about me once they got to know me, and after that, it was really the only thing people saw.

I couldn't really blame people for anything. If I wasn't like this, then I probably wouldn't know how to treat someone who was a shapeshifter, either.

Only, I was like this, and I did know.

And right now, I didn't want to feel like a freak the way I always did. Right now, I wanted something new. Something fresh. Right now, I wanted him to treat me like I was the dirtiest damn girl in the world.

"You're a good tiger."

"Convince me to go run with you," I said, jutting my chin forward. I wanted him to kiss me again. Wanted him to do other things again.

Kapono grinned, grabbed me by the waist, and tugged me flush against his body.

When he kissed me again, I was completely convinced.

6

Kapono

Oh, she was fantastic. I knew the moment she'd decided that I had convinced her to come running with me. I could tell the second she was ready because she practically melted against me. She opened her lips slightly, inviting me into her mouth, and I took full advantage of the situation.

It wasn't every day you met someone willing to pretend to be your wife.

It wasn't every day they were as gorgeous as Darla.

Finally, reluctantly, I pulled away.

"Come with me."

"Where?"

"Everywhere," I whispered.

She looked shy for just a moment before she decided to be brave. She nodded.

"I'll do it. Let's go."

I paused for a moment. I was about to strip out of the rest of my clothing and take off into the woods. As a cat, I loved shifting and going running and exploring with all of my friends, but I suddenly wondered if Darla and I had the same idea.

"Darling?"

She looked up at me, eyes bright.

"Have you ever done this before?"

"I've shifted before."

"Because you wanted to?"

Hesitation.

A pause.

There it was.

There was something she hadn't told me, something she didn't want me to know. I was probably overthinking it, which was fair enough, but I'd been a bartender for a long time. When you waited on people who were drinking, you very quickly learned to read their body language before you listened to their words.

The woman who came in downing shots for "liquid courage" when it came to actually meeting up on her blind date was saying something very different than the woman downing shots at a bridal shower. The guy in the corner sipping on rum and Cokes gave off a very different vibe than the frat bros who ordered rounds "for the bar" and then tried to skip out on the tab.

As the co-owner of the bar, I'd had to become very good at reading people very fast, and one thing that intrigued and confused me about Darla was the fact that although she was a shapeshifter, she didn't seem to be very comfortable talking about it.

Even now, she hesitated when it came time to actually shift and take off running with me. Now, maybe she was just nervous about me seeing her naked for the first time. That was understandable. The two of us could have waited a little while before we shifted in front of each other. Shifting in front of someone new was always a little challenging just because you hadn't seen them naked so you didn't know what to expect.

With Darla, I was excited about that.

Most shifters had this unspoken rule that we never said anything negative about anyone's body. Just like humans who came in different shapes and sizes, shifters did the same thing. Some shifters were big and some were small. Some were strong and some were weak.

Some were fast.

Some were...well, not so fast.

There was something else, though.

"Darla?"

"I've never shifted because I wanted to," she said slowly.

"Never?"

"I've never been given the choice."

"Why not?"

She looked up at me sharply. "You can't just ask people about their sordid past, Kapono."

I shrugged. "Sure, I can. I'm your husband, remember?"

"Pretend husband," she corrected me. "And I'm not so sure that being my pretend husband is actually a very good cover. Actually, I really think that people are going to figure this out."

"There's no way."

"How can you be so sure?"

"Look, people see what they want to see, and what people want to see is that I'm married and settling down. Hell, I'll take you to my mom's place tomorrow."

"You'd lie to your mother?"

Out of everything I'd said, that was the thing that stood out to Darla. She didn't want me to lie to my mom. Interesting. So, family was important to her. I could understand that.

"I would."

"Why?"

"Wouldn't you lie to yours?"

"My mom is dead."

"Your dad, then."

"Dead."

"Do you have any family who isn't dead?"

She paused for a moment and then shook her head.

"What happened?"

"Another personal question."

"What can I say? I'm a personal sort of guy."

"I can see that."

"Take off your shirt," I told her.

"What?"

"We can get personal later. You don't want to talk. That's totally fine. We can talk later. Right now, take off the shirt so we can go run."

I walked past her, pushing my way out of the door. I wasn't going to give her a hard time anymore. I wanted this thing between us to be something that was mutually beneficial for both of us. I couldn't really do that if she was scared.

I wasn't sure why Darla was suddenly so important to me. She was Jim's responsibility, actually, but it wasn't like Jim had a good way to hide her. He was married to a man and they had no children. He couldn't say something like, "oh, she's my long-lost daughter." People would know if Jim had a kid.

Besides, she was too delicious to pass up.

Once I was outside, I finished stripping down with my back to the house. I could feel her eyes on me as I got naked. I liked it, though. I liked knowing that she was watching me take off my clothing. I wondered if she liked the view as much as I liked showing off for her.

Damn, if she wasn't the best thing that had happened to me in absolute years.

I tossed my clothes over my shoulder toward the porch. I heard them land on the ground. I'd missed. Still, I didn't turn around. Instead, I shifted into my tiger form as I walked lazily away from the house and hoped that she'd take the hint.

I didn't want this to be uncomfortable for her.

I wanted this to be fun for her.

We could see well in the dark, especially when we were in our tiger bodies. We had excellent eyesight even in our human forms, though, and that was something I had always really appreciated. Now, I liked that we were under the cover of darkness because it was going to give her a little bit of a chance to change into her tiger self without the fear of embarrassment.

Not that I wouldn't love to look at her.

I would.

Darla was lovely and sweet with just the right amount of attitude. I walked slowly away from the house. In a minute, she'd shift on her own and run to catch up with me. That was okay.

I wasn't sure where my new patient attitude had come from, but I did know that if I wasn't careful, I was going to become very addicted to Darla. People in Wishville viewed me as random and chaotic. They viewed me as someone who was a little wild and a little unpredictable.

That was why the idea of me suddenly appearing with a wife was so believable to them.

People here knew that I was a little bit strange, so the choices I made reflected that.

With Darla, I didn't want to be weird or random or wild.

With her, I wanted to offer peace.

I had a feeling that Darla hadn't been offered any sort of haven or place to belong in a very, very long time, so when I heard her clothes hit the ground and the gentle *whoosh* of her shifting into her tiger form, I couldn't help the delight I felt inside.

She trusted me enough to shift.

7

Darla

I didn't know it was this possible to feel this alive. When he'd invited me to run with him, I didn't really know what was going to happen. At first, I thought that running with him was something that would feel strangely personal, and on that level, it had.

But it was more than that.

For the first time in a very, very long time, I felt free.

I felt happy.

I felt content.

For the very first time, it was like nothing could stop me because I was strong and powerful. I finally felt like I was starting to believe that.

I'd gone through a lot during the time I'd lived with the magician. Most of my memories were not exactly fun. Not exactly things I'd want anyone else to ever have to experience. Still, I was starting to get used to the way life looked on the outside. I was starting to get used to the idea that there might be more to life than *hiding*.

And it started tonight.

I ran through the woods. If I had been able to, I would have laughed. It was actually very strange to not be able to laugh at this moment. Laughing was such a natural feeling, a natural expression, that I really thought I should have been doing just that.

Only, I wasn't.

Still, I felt carefree and calm as we made our way through the darkness. With the stars and the moonlight, as well as my shifter sight, I could see Kapono's sleek body moving across the grass fields that led to the forests of Rawr County.

There were a lot.

One of the things I loved so much about Colorado was just that there were so many trees and mountains and hills. There were an incredible number of places where we could just *be*.

And I liked that.

As a kid, I'd always felt the need to run. I'd *loved* running. I'd loved being outdoors and climbing trees and just feeling at peace.

Then my parents died and I'd gone to live with my aunt. If she was a shapeshifter, I didn't know it because she'd never said. I wished she had told me who my parents really were. I'd never learned whether both of my parents were tigers or whether just my dad was. I didn't know. Aunt Susan had been strict in many ways, but never cruel. When she'd passed away, I'd been so heartbroken that I'd basically just down emotionally.

And then I'd shifted.

It had been a strange sort of feeling. The grief that wrapped around me had been postponed for years. I'd put off grieving for my parents because I didn't think I was supposed to or allowed to, but not actually processing what happened until my guardian died meant that the grief I felt over Susan's death was tripled.

And that was when I'd changed.

I pushed the thought out of my mind, though. Instead of worrying about the past, I just thought about running with

Kapono. I raced and felt the wind on my face, and I imagined that I lived in a world where nothing hurt.

Together, the two of us ran.

I couldn't hear anything except the sound of our paws hitting the ground as we barreled forward. We moved very, very fast. Faster than I thought possible. Faster than I thought would have been okay. We just ran.

And while I was running, it was like nothing else mattered.

My stress and my sadness just faded away and I finally, finally started to feel free. It felt like this was the first time I was just letting go of everything I worried about, everything that made me feel lost or scared or upset.

And I just *moved*.

I finally started to feel like everything was going to be okay, and I knew that it was because of him.

Because of Kapono.

Because of the kind, strange man I'd met in the bar.

Now, Kapono led the way. I followed close behind. Each turn he made was like another adventure being brought forth in front of me. Each turn made me feel like I was flying. Soon we were racing as the night continued, until finally, we started to slow down. I was glad because I was getting tired. I imagined he was used to this kind of movement, though. He was probably slowing down just for me.

Then I realized where we were, and my jaw dropped open.

We were standing together at the top of a cliff overlooking the city.

He shifted back into his human form and dropped to the ground. Then he scooted until he was sitting at the edge of the cliff. He didn't say anything. Didn't ask me to shift back. He just waited.

And I watched him.

Kapono was handsome. He had a couple of scars on his back and a few on his shoulders, but nothing unexpected. It wasn't like he had been horrifically or brutally marred in any way. Instead, it seemed like he was the kind of person who had lived an adventurous sort of life.

I wondered what the story of those scars was.

Had he been a cyclist?

A runner?

An avid tree climber?

Maybe he'd been the kind of teenager who got hurt skateboarding.

Maybe he'd gotten in fights.

I resisted the urge to walk over, shifter, and kneel behind him, but it was hard. I wanted to press my fingers to his skin and run my palms over each little scar, each little freckle, each little mark that made him who he was.

Kapono finally turned around and looked at me. He gestured to the space beside him, as if I didn't see it.

"Sit."

I didn't move.

Couldn't.

All of a sudden, I found myself freezing in place because I still wasn't sure where I stood with him.

I was so very attracted to Kapono, but I also knew that a guy like him couldn't really be interested in someone like me.

Besides, he wasn't asking me for anything.

Not yet, anyway.

In the past, the people who had captured me had seemed like they were trying to help me at first. They'd offered me shelter and a place to stay in exchange for being a part of their magic show. It wasn't until later, when I'd tried to leave, that things had gone south.

I didn't think Kapono was like them, though, and I couldn't pinpoint why I felt that way.

I stood where I was and watched him. He cocked his head and smiled gently. Without another word, he gestured to me and patted the ground beside him. I wasn't sure if he wanted me to sit down in my tiger form or if he wanted me to change, so for right now, I just moved my tiger self beside him, and I lowered myself to the ground.

And then I closed my eyes.

8

Kapono

I reached for the beautiful creature beside me and started petting her softly. Oh, she was a delight. The sound that Darla made was nothing short of the world's most perfect purr, and I loved it. I loved all of this.

I wasn't sure what tigers were supposed to do in situations like this. It was rare that people I dated actually shifted with me or that we hung out together in shifter form. In the past, shifting and running had been something I did with my friends and even my brother, but this...

This just felt *right*.

There were a lot of things about Darla that felt right.

"There's my good girl," I murmured softly. She looked so sweet here, so serene. It was nice to see her feeling at peace after experiencing so much chaos in her life. I didn't know everything she'd gone through, and I probably never would know everything her experiences entailed, but I knew that she'd been in trouble and I knew that right now, in this moment, she was safe.

She was safe with me.

Her eyes fluttered open, and she turned and looked at me, but didn't shift back, and I didn't ask her to. I knew that she needed this moment to truly feel like she belonged.

And to feel safe.

I watched my tiger as she continued to relax. Muscle by muscle, the tension fled her body and soon she was practically melting into the ground with comfort and relaxation.

"I don't know what you've been through," I whispered to her, "but I know what it's like to be scared."

I knew it far too well.

It was something that most people knew about *a little*. Most people had experienced being scared of the dark when your mother insisted you were too old for a night light. Most of us had experienced fear when we'd had to speak in front of our middle school auditorium during a play. A few of us had even experienced the fear that wrapped around you when you were home alone for the first time and were *certain* you'd heard a noise in the basement.

This, though...

The fear that Darla felt was different.

There was really no other way to describe it.

She still didn't shift back, but that was okay. I was good at talking. I was good at listening, too. Years of running the bar had gotten me there. People would say a lot once they got talking, and usually, all it took to get people talking was to be quiet for a little while.

Now Darla was the one being quiet, and suddenly, I found myself blurting out something I never shared with anyone.

Ever.

"My brother died."

The purring stopped, but I kept talking. Now that I'd started, I wasn't sure that I was going to be able to stop. My hand didn't leave her head. I kept petting her with one palm while my other rested on my knee. Looking out over the wilderness made the moment feel peaceful, and it gave me the strength to talk about Grant and how much I missed him.

How much I needed him.

There was a part of me that wished I'd stop missing my brother one day, but there was another part, a deeper part, that appreciated the pain that accompanied this longing. When you missed someone, it meant that they had been special to you. When you craved their presence, it just meant that you adored them. There were so many ways that Grant had made my life better and now that he was gone, I felt like there was a hole in my heart.

"We were sixteen. Twins. Both tigers, of course." I swallowed hard. It had been over a decade and I still hadn't gotten over it. Now, quickly approaching thirty years old, I felt like I should have been over it.

I wasn't.

I still hadn't stopped missing him.

Hadn't stopped picking up my phone to call him with a funny joke I'd heard.

Hadn't stopped turning to see if he was laughing only to realize he'd been dead for years.

My heart hurt.

Grant had been incredible. People always liked to talk about the fact that twins had "so much" in common, and that had been true for us. We'd had this incredible bond that nobody had known what to do with and nobody had been able to break.

Well, it was broken now, and I still mourned that loss.

"The two of us did everything together," I continued. It was hard not to get teary-eyed as I thought about it. I'd shed plenty of tears over my brother and I knew I had plenty more to shed.

It never really did get easier.

Everyone liked to think that when you lost someone, you were sad for a little while and then you felt better. Humans and shifters alike were not exempt from the reality that once you lost someone, you felt their absence for years. You felt it during holiday dinners when someone told a lame story and you felt it on rainy mornings when you planned to ask them if they'd like to watch a movie, only the person wasn't there.

They were never going to be *there* again.

"He was hit by a car," I said. I stared out at the vast wilderness. My brother and I had spent so much time racing through these mountains and playing in these forests. The world had really felt like our own. "Nobody ever found out who did it. Shifters are supposed to be these big, strong creatures, but we're also real people. We might not be human, but we're real, and losing him felt like someone carved out part of my heart."

I wasn't the only one who had felt like that, either.

"Part of the reason I'm so unpredictable now is that after my brother died, I stopped trying to please people. I started trying to live in a way that made me happy. Other people don't have to understand. Didn't have to understand. I miss my brother a lot, and I know that he was always the type of guy who wanted to have a little bit of excitement in his life."

That was part of the reason I'd started the bar. Jim and Kellan were a few years older than me. They were like big brothers when I'd been growing up, and they saw what it was like for me after Grant passed. They knew I was lonely, and when I dropped out of art school, Jim and I decided to launch the bar together. Kellan had always been more of a musician than a bartender, but he still helped out from time to time. He was also the one who had encouraged us to work on finishing up the basement. He had an idea of hosting musicians down there on the weekends, and I thought that was a damn cool idea.

I could feel Darla's eyes on me as I looked out over the cliffs. Grant would have loved her. I might not have known a lot of things, but I definitely knew that about my brother. He would have absolutely, completely adored her.

"That sounds really hard."

I looked over. I hadn't even realized that she'd changed back. I'd been so caught up in my thoughts that I hadn't realized I was no longer rubbing her soft tiger fur, but her curly hair instead. Darla was watching me carefully, but not moving. I appreciated her gentleness in this moment.

"It was."

"I know what it feels like to lose people you care about," she told me.

I knew that.

I knew she'd been through loss.

There was something about losing someone you loved that changed you. It was like the pain morphed you somehow. It became a part of you and even when you tried to hide it, that ache was always there. That loneliness never really dissipated.

And it did more than just become part of you. It was like a beacon, signaling to other people who were hurting just how much pain you were in. That was the reason we always seemed so good at finding other people who were also hurting.

Once you were in pain, you could find others.

"Your parents." That was my guess as to who she had lost.

"My parents and then my aunt. She's the one who basically raised me. I was so young when my folks died that she was really the person who gave me the most care during my life. After she died, I was so sad that I couldn't handle it."

And why should she have had to?

I hated knowing that she had faced her aunt's passing alone. This sweet, wonderful woman didn't need to be dealing with loss like that on her own.

No one did.

We might not have been human, but we weren't meant to be solitary creatures. We needed each other. That was the only way to get through life, in my opinion.

"That's a normal feeling." With death, there was no such thing as a "wrong" or even "unexpected" feeling. I'd been to counselors over the years who had drilled this into my head.

There was no such thing as a "bad" feeling when it came to handling grief.

"That was when I shifted," she said.

Wait. What?

"You'd never shifted before?"

"Never."

"How old were you?"

"19," she whispered. "I was supposed to be getting ready to go off to college, but instead, I was discovering that I was a shapeshifter."

She'd been a late bloomer. That was a little unusual, but not as unusual as not knowing at all. Then I realized what had happened.

"Did your aunt not know you were a shifter?" Or had she just not said anything about it? I wasn't sure which would be worse. If Darla's parents had died before they got to tell her that she was a shifter, it made sense that her aunt might not share that information. And the fact that she'd been through so much trauma could have caused her to basically go through a late shifter puberty.

"She and my mom were sisters. I think maybe just my dad was a shifter."

It was possible for a human and a shifter to have shifter kids. In fact, that was the way it normally worked. I'd only heard of rare cases where the baby would be human and unable to shift, but it was strange that nobody had taken the time to tell her before they passed.

Shifters had a lot going on in our lives, but we also tended to really look forward to the fact that we would be able to shift one day.

I couldn't imagine what it had felt like to *not* know.

Grant and I had both been very excited to learn how to shift. It was something we'd spent years dreaming about and thinking about. In fact, it was one of the things we'd both teased each other about. We each wanted to be the one to shift first.

"What did you do when it happened?"

"When I shifted?"

I nodded.

"I freaked out," she whispered. "I couldn't figure out how to change back. That was when I met Dwayne." She took a deep breath. "And Mike."

Instantly, I hated them. Without her saying another word, I knew that these were the guys responsible for making her life hell for so very long. They'd hurt her. I didn't know how, and I didn't need all of the details, but I knew enough. I knew that they were the reason she was here.

They were the reason my sweet Darla was afraid.

"Tell me what happened," I whispered. The sun was going to come up soon, and the two of us would go back to my place. We'd crawl under the blankets and sleep the day away, and she'd be safe. She wouldn't have to do a single damn thing except sleep and rest and know that she was so very, very important.

She was special.

And I really was crazy about her.

"They found me in the park," she said. "I was hanging out at the edge of the woods, and I couldn't figure out what to do, but they knew what to do."

Of course, they did. They were probably assholes just looking for easy prey.

"They talked me down and got me to change back into my regular, normal self," she whispered. "At first, I thought everything was going to be okay."

I already knew that it wouldn't.

I already knew that whatever happened next, the story was about to get really, really sad.

"Then they grabbed me, and they took me, and I knew after that nothing would ever be the same again."

9

Darla

He started kissing my cheeks.

I hadn't even realized that I'd been crying until I felt his kisses on my skin. They were soft at first, and gentle, and then he reached my mouth and that was when lust overpowered my sadness. I kissed him back eagerly. He tasted like heaven, but my heart hurt like hell. Reliving the past was a terrible idea.

Maybe Kapono could help me forget.

I doubted that I'd ever *really* forget. I wouldn't be able to let go entirely. Who could? When something traumatic happened, it changed who you were. It changed the way that you viewed people and the world around you. It altered everything.

As if reading my mind, Kapono pulled away and gripped my shoulders.

"I will never let them hurt you again," he said. There was a certain firmness to his voice: a ferocity I hadn't expected.

"Never?"

"Never," he repeated. "They will never get you, Darla. No matter how long you stay here, they will never find you. I give you my word."

And I believed him.

I wasn't under any sort of impression that Kapono was a safe man or a gentle guy, but he was honorable. The fact that people in Rawr County trusted him meant a lot to me. When we'd been at One More Howl, a ton of people had congratulated us on our "wedding," and strangely enough, they'd all believed the story.

More than that, they'd been *happy*.

Every single person I talked to had been so very happy that Kapono had found love, and that really did speak volumes. It let me know that he was the kind of guy who spread kindness and happiness, and he had a reputation as being a damn good person.

He started kissing me again, and my heart began to soar.

Even through my tears, he was kissing away the pain and silently reminding me that I was going to be okay.

I wanted more than being okay, though.

I wanted him.

When he'd said he would tell people we were married, I didn't know what to expect. Finding myself at the edge of a cliff with him wasn't really on my list, but the attraction between us had been instant, and I was too old to feel like denying myself these simple pleasures in life.

So, I pulled him closer to me, and I felt myself just *let go*.

I wasn't afraid.

I wasn't scared.

I was ready.

For this.

For him.

For all of it.

His hands explored my body as I tried to do the same to his. His whole body was hard, like he'd been carved from stone. It wasn't fair that he got to look so thick and fit, but I could tell by the way he was nipping at my neck that he liked my figure just fine.

I wasn't embarrassed about being curvy, but I also didn't really expect people to like me. The fact that he very much *did* made me feel incredible.

When Kapono's hands reached my breasts, he paused for a moment. Then his eyes locked on mine and he nodded.

"Perfect."

There it was.

One little word.

One sweetly, carefully whispered word, and I was done for.

I knew in that moment that no matter what came next, I would never be the same. No matter what happened after tonight, I was going to be different.

I was going to be changed.

I was going to be filled with a beautiful sort of confidence that nothing would be able to shatter.

And oh, I was happy.

He palmed my breasts, bouncing them gently in his hands.

"These are so fucking lovely," he told me.

"Thank you." I bit my lip. I wasn't sure what to say. Not right now. The scent of arousal wrapped around us. We were both excited for this moment: both ready.

We both needed this.

He didn't say anything else as he held me there. We were still close to the edge of the cliff, and I might have been a shifter, but I still didn't have wings, so we moved a short distance away. There was a patch there filled with clover and flowers, and he spread me out on my back before making his way down my body.

Kisses.

Touches.

Tiny little nips.

Kapono seemed to work my body like magic. He made my heart feel like it was flying. I closed my eyes as he touched me, and I just *felt*. I allowed myself to just be completely swept up in the moment because it was the most peace I'd felt in ages.

And it wasn't what I expected to feel today.

What I expected to feel was afraid.

Nervous.

Scared.

I didn't.

Instead, I felt like everything in my life had led me here, to him. It was like everything I'd ever done had culminated in this moment.

He made his way down my body, kissing and teasing me. When he reached the apex of my thighs, he smiled up at me as he began licking me, tasting me, and I couldn't keep my eyes open anymore. I closed them and allowed myself to just feel.

Allowed myself to just be totally present in the moment.

The sun was starting to come up, which meant we were being cast in the softest orange glow. I wanted to lie still as he touched me, but I couldn't. Instead, my hands were on his shoulders, in his hair, and finally, on my own breasts.

And then I came.

An orgasm was supposed to be something you got to experience whenever you wanted, but as someone who had rarely been alone for years, it still felt like a strange and exotic treat. The magic coursed through my veins, and I felt like I was floating.

Kapono wasn't supposed to happen.

I wasn't supposed to fall for someone like him, and it was crazy to think that we were doing this after we'd only just met, but we were, and I was…

Glad.

Then he was over me.

"You're perfect," he said again.

And then Kapono slid inside of me.

I reached for him, pulling him close. I was kissing his cheek and running my hands down his back. My legs wrapped around him, and in that moment, I knew that nothing was ever going to be the same for me.

I'd been so very scared for so long. I'd been afraid and in hiding for years, but right now, everything was changing.

Right now, my entire world was becoming something else.

Something better.

Something new.

When Kapono came, he shuddered. He whispered my name and slid his tongue over my lips, and I knew right then that coming to Rawr County had been the best possible thing in my life.

It was the greatest decision I'd ever made.

And he was…

Well, he was the best pretend husband I could have hoped for.

10

Kapono

When I woke up in the early afternoon, I sat up sharply and looked over at the person next to me. She was still here. Darla hadn't run.

I'd half-expected her to, to be honest. She had been so afraid and scared, and I'd felt the same way. I wasn't really used to giving it up to someone I'd just met, but I also wasn't really used to feeling this strange addiction when I looked over at her.

She was gently snoring, sprawled out on her tummy. With the windows open and the sun spilling in the tiny room, she looked like something out of a painting.

I was so used to waking up alone that having someone here with me felt awkward and strange, but only for a brief moment. Then, as I remembered all of the wonderful things the two of us had done, it started to feel good.

Really good.

"Hey," I murmured, reaching for Darla's back. I stroked her soft skin, teasing her with my fingertips. I ran my hand down her back and up again, gently massaging her. Oh, she was so perfect.

I only hoped that she knew that.

When the two of us had made love near the cliffs, I had been surprised. Not that I hadn't wanted to. Obviously, I'd really, really wanted to.

I just didn't enter this "fake marriage" with any sort of expectations. I didn't do this because I wanted something or thought I was going to get something.

Instead, I did it because it felt right.

She felt right.

"Good morning," she whispered, and then her eyes fluttered open. She smiled at me and then rolled onto her back, revealing her naked body. My hands were on her breasts before I could stop myself: gently massaging, gently touching her.

"It's the afternoon," I reminded her. "We slept the day away."

"Good. I think we deserved it," Darla smiled at me. She didn't look embarrassed or shy about what we'd done. She just seemed happy.

"How'd you sleep?"

"Terribly," she told me. "Someone wouldn't let me sleep."

"Look," I laughed, reaching for her. "You're far too pretty to let sleep."

It was true that I hadn't given her much space. Instead, I'd kissed her. Touched her. Held her. I'd made her feel just as incredible as she made me feel. I'd taken full advantage of the fact that people thought we were married and that they already thought we were sleeping together.

So, we slept together, and it was damn fantastic.

She was fun.

There was a sweetness to Darla that I assumed she didn't let people see very often.

It was there, lurking just beneath the surface of what she was presenting to the world.

She'd told me a little bit about what had happened to her. I didn't know why she'd stayed with her captors or why she hadn't tried to run before, but it didn't matter. The only thing that really mattered was that she was here with me now and the two of us were going to take good care of her.

"Did you have fun?" Darla asked, almost shyly.

"So much fun."

It wasn't a lie or an exaggeration.

"Me too. We should do this again sometime," she laughed.

"I have some free time," I glanced at an invisible watch on my wrist. "Right about now. Interested?"

"Very," she smiled and reached for me, and I knew it was going to be a very good afternoon indeed.

*

After an hour of making love, we were both exhausted and needed a break. That was something I never thought I'd think about sex, but it was time. We just needed a little rest: just something to get us through. The two of us headed back to the bar and got my car. Darla followed me back to the house where we snacked and drank some water and did a little baking. Then it was time to get going.

Just after dinnertime, I took Darla over to my mom's place. The tiny brick house sat just a few blocks from the bar. Despite its close location, my mother wasn't a drinker, so she rarely, if ever, came to see me at work. The house was a single story with lots of windows and a small porch with a wooden rocker on it.

Darla turned to me and raised an eyebrow. I hadn't told her where we were going.

"What are we doing here?"

"I told you I'd introduce you to my mom. She'll be happy to meet you."

"Are you serious? We aren't actually married, though," Darla whispered. She looked a little anxious and kind of scared, but I just shrugged.

"It'll be fine. You'll see." My mom wasn't going to care.

"Don't you need to get to the bar?"

"Don't worry," I reached out and cupped her cheek. Then I kissed her. "Sloan is going to open. My bouncer, Brock, will be there to help her."

"Are you sure they can handle it?"

"He's an elephant shifter, love. He can handle it."

She stared at me, blinking.

"What?"

"Elephant shifter."

"How is that even possible?"

"How is any of this possible?" I asked her gently. It was something I was certain every shifter asked themselves. How was it even possible that we could magically transform ourselves into something else? How was it possible that we could somehow, magically just be *able* to do this?

"It shouldn't be."

"Maybe not," I murmured. "But I think it's kind of nice."

"What was it like for you?" Darla asked me. "You know, growing up in a place where shifters existed? Was it weird or was it nice?"

"I've never known anything else." I couldn't really give her a real answer on that level. As kids, my brother and I loved talking about the day we'd be able to change into our tiger selves. We hadn't been able to until we were ten, and even then, we'd been considered "early" shifters. It was kind of cool and had given us bragging rights among the other tigers we liked to hang out with.

"I'm a little jealous," she said.

"You shouldn't be."

"Just of the fact that you knew there were others," she explained.

"Being alone must have been tough," I admitted. I couldn't imagine just randomly shifting into someone – something – else one day. Poor Darla must have been petrified.

"I figured it out okay," she shrugged.

But she shouldn't have had to.

She shouldn't have had to deal with it alone.

"Let's go inside," I took her hand and squeezed it gently. "Let's go drink some tea and eat some cookies and let's pretend that everything's normal, okay?"

She nodded. "I'd like that."

Together, we headed up to the front door where my mother was already standing. She hadn't been expecting me, but she had shifter hearing, so she'd definitely heard the car pulling up and she certainly knew when an unexpected visitor was arriving.

"Kapono?" Mom looked at me through the screen door. She pushed it open and smiled at Darla. "You brought a friend. Nice to meet you. I'm Kia."

"Nice to meet you," Darla smiled. The scent of nervousness permeated the air. She was uncomfortable with the situation, but any non-shifter would never know. She had her shoulders back and her head up. She was ready for the situation, no matter what it brought. I was proud of her. "I'm Darla."

"Mom, she's my wife," I said firmly. I was never going to tell my mother that Darla and I weren't legally married. Ever. Besides, after the squeal my mom let out, I knew that we were going to be good.

"Are you serious? Darla, get in here!" Mom started laughing and somehow, the three of us managed to get inside and situated on the living room couches with a pitcher of sun tea and a plate of sugar cookies. That was when Mom really smiled.

"She's always wanted me to get married," I explained to Darla.

"I've always wanted you to be happy," Mom corrected.

That much, at least, was true. My mother and I had relationship that could be tricky. We were both stubborn people. We were both a little too confident sometimes.

After Grant died and then, a few years later, my dad, Mom had focused more on finding her own happiness and less on worrying about me. That was one of the reasons she didn't complain that her son hung out and ran a bar with his friend. She just wanted me to be okay.

"Well, I'm glad that you're happy for us," Darla said politely. "I know that this must seem kind of sudden..." Her voice trailed off and she looked over at me. I knew exactly what she was thinking. She wanted to know why the hell everyone in Rawr County seemed so eager to believe that I'd taken a bride.

"I was a very eligible bachelor," I told Darla. "That's why no one is surprised you snatched me up."

"Is that so?" Mom laughed.

"It's so. We both know it."

Mom smiled. She asked Darla where she was from and what she liked to do. Darla did a great job answering questions and finding some common ground with my mom. They both liked art, so they talked about drawing and painting, and I just relaxed and watched them. Darla left out the bits about her being captured and held against her will for some time, but Mom didn't seem to catch on that there was anything else strange about the situation.

By the time we left, Darla had eaten half a dozen cookies and I'd had twice that many. Mom, somehow, had the self-control of a saint because she hadn't eaten any at all.

"Wait," Mom said. She held up her phone. "We need to get a picture before you go."

Darla froze. We hadn't talked about this because I didn't even think it would come up. We couldn't have Mom taking pictures of Darla right now, though. Maybe in the future, it would be an option, but right now, we couldn't have that.

"Mom, Darla and I don't really want any pictures on social media right now." That was fair enough. A lot of people didn't want their pictures posted online.

Mom just waved her hand. "It's just for me, dear. I won't be posting it."

Darla looked over at me and bit her lip. I knew she wanted to refuse, but if we did, it was going to seem even stranger than us getting married randomly.

"Promise?" I asked Mom. "No Facebook? No Insta?"

"Cross my heart," she smiled.

"It's okay," I told Darla, squeezing her hand. She hesitated, but then nodded. The two of us spent a few minutes posing for my mom in various positions until she was happy. Then it was finally time to leave. The two of us headed to the car and slipped inside.

"Well, what did you think?" I asked as we pulled away. My mom stood on the porch so she and Darla could wave at each other as we left, and when we rounded the bend, she leaned back and closed her eyes.

"I liked her."

"Me too."

"She's really nice, Kapono."

"I completely agree."

And she'd always been there for me. No matter what I'd ever gone through, Mom had come through 100%. She was always there for me, always ready to lend a hand. Always ready to help.

"I don't know if we should be doing this to her," Darla whispered.

"We aren't doing anything to her."

Only, that wasn't quite true. We were lying. We were being tricky and deceitful. I didn't care about any of that because in my mind, it was for a good reason. We were doing this to protect her and keep her safe.

We weren't doing this to impress other people.

"She's going to be hurt," Darla's voice was so quiet that I almost couldn't hear her, but I hated the way that she was right.

My mother was already texting me about the visit. My phone was buzzing every few seconds in my pocket, and I knew that no matter how things with me and Darla went, someone was going to get hurt.

Maybe everyone.

11

Darla

As it turned out, Wishville wasn't really what I thought it was going to be like.

I had figured it would be a place where I could hide out as I tried to rebuild some semblance of an identity, but the town itself was actually very idyllic and actually very comforting.

In some ways, being in Wishville was like finding hope. It almost felt like coming home. Even though that was cheesy and perhaps even shocking to some people, the truth was that I'd never really felt like I belonged...until now.

Now, I finally felt like I belonged.

I finally felt like I had a place that needed me.

I finally felt like I had a place where I could just *be*.

A couple of days passed. Kia dropped by with cookies and with a recommendation (which may have been a request, I couldn't really tell) that we hold a reception at some point. She thought it would be nice to have one in the bar where all of our friends and Kapono's relatives could come. I'd shared that my family had passed away, and Kia had been kind enough not to ask too many questions about that.

Kapono had been open to the idea of a reception or just a big party in general, and that had pleased his mother. She'd darted off to make plans with her friends, and I had been happy to not have to participate very much in the planning stuff.

Today, it was just Kapono and me.

"What's for lunch?" I asked, glancing over at Kapono. In his white tee and his too tight jeans, he looked handsome. He was the kind of guy I could really get on board with being with. I knew that this wasn't the way I was supposed to feel about him. After all, he was just some guy who was doing me a favor – albeit a big one - but still.

I did feel that way.

He was someone who intrigued me.

"Anything you want," he said.

"What?"

"For lunch. Anything you want."

"Anything?"

"Whatever you like."

After a short discussion, we decided on sandwiches from a little cafe just a short walk from the bar where he worked. We found ourselves seated in the back with two overstuffed turkey sandwiches sitting right in front of us. As I looked at the food, my stomach rumbled. It had been far too long since I'd just sat and eaten sandwiches with someone I cared about.

"To us," he said.

"So," he said.

"So," I said.

It seemed like we'd talked about so very many different things that it felt like we'd known each other for years.

"Why Wishville?" Kapono smiled gently as he asked me. I looked at Kapono carefully. There was so much to take in about him. At first glance he looked like any sort of normal man, but when you looked a little bit deeper, it was easier to see just how much more there was.

"You know why I'm here." We'd talked about it. I'd shared with him. He knew I'd escaped. I'd had so many chances over the years and I'd never taken them. My captors had promised that if I ever left, I would be worthless. They convinced me that I was the only one of my kind and that there was something seriously wrong with me. They said they were protecting me, and for a long time, I believed it.

They told me that if I ever left, I'd be branded as a freak.

Then I realized that I already was.

It was after one of the magic shows when I happened to hear people talking about the performance, and that was the day I realized people didn't come to watch me because I was cool or special.

They viewed me as a monster.

And that was all it took.

I'd left the next day and I'd never looked back. I still battled with the idea that I was worthless, and I knew that I would for a long, long time, but I was free.

And with Kapono's help, I was starting to realize that I was very much *not* worthless.

Kapono shook his head. His eyes were bright, but his lips were pressed together. Because he didn't want to say anything. Not just yet. He was doing the thing where he waited for me. That way I would be forced to speak.

"It's all thanks to Georgia."

"Why would she send you here, though?"

I knew he was starting to like me. It was impossible for us not to like each other. If we'd been smart, we wouldn't have slept together, but we had, and there was no going back now.

From this moment on, whatever happened between the two of us was basically fate, and it was strange because I still hadn't met Jim. I still hadn't met George's friend. I didn't really know what the deal was with Georgia and Jim or why she thought this was the kind of place I should be. But as I looked at Kapono, I knew that whatever came next was going to be what was meant to be.

"She trusts Jim."

"And you could trust me, you know," he said gently.

I knew he wasn't trying to be a dick. He wasn't trying to push me. Not really. Not too hard. Unfortunately, I didn't really feel like I could give him anything more than I already had offered. The truth was, Kapono didn't really know very much about me. And that was the way I liked it. I wanted Wishville to be a fresh start. I didn't want it to be a place where I just relived and rehashed the same old stuff.

I shook my head.

"It's heavy."

"I know," Kapono told me, "but maybe that's why we should talk about it."

I picked up my sandwich. I took a little bite. It was good. To be honest, it was quite possibly the best sandwich I'd had in a really long time. Maybe ever. I couldn't really explain to anyone just how amazing the sandwich was. Because there was no way that they would ever actually believe me.

There was something about a sandwich that brought me back to my childhood. My mom had never believed in those simple, easy peanut butter and jelly sandwich type things. Instead, she had always cooked me something fancier, something a little bit bigger. She'd throw some sort of me on some sort of bread or roll and then add lots and lots of vegetables. It was like heaven. It was like magic. It was like everything I'd ever wanted anything to be and then it was a little bit better.

Kapono's own sandwich was untouched.

"Aren't you going to eat that?" I asked him, pointing at it.

"I will soon." Kapono shook his head. "But right now, I need a little bit of honesty from you."

"You're asking too much of me."

"I don't think I'm asking enough of you, to be honest. Look, I'm staking my whole reputation on you. I told everyone that I married you because I know that you need this."

And because we were attracted to each other.

And because he wanted an adventure as much as I wanted to be safe.

I had known that there would come a time when we'd be forced to have this conversation, but I didn't know it was going to be today. I hadn't *wanted* it to be today.

What I'd wanted was a little bit of time where the two of us could just keep playing pretend. I wanted to keep imagining that we had this sweet, wonderful world where everything was normal and okay and lovely.

Only, that wasn't our reality.

Also, he wasn't done talking.

I picked at the pickles on my sandwich as I listened to him.

"And I know that you need someone to help you. I know that you need a little bit of time and a little bit of freedom. I get that honey. I really do."

The thing about Kapono was that he didn't really get it. He'd grown up in a world where being a shapeshifter was okay. He had been raised by people who accepted him and loved him.

I had never gotten that. I had never been given the chance to find that sort of piece. What I had been given was the opportunity to realize that I couldn't trust anyone.

"Look, the world isn't safe for people like us."

Kapono cocked his head considering this.

"What do you mean?"

"Well, think about it."

He looked like he was thinking about it.

"When did you find out that you were a shapeshifter?" I asked him even though I already knew. He and his twin had been so very happy that they were shifters. They'd been able to change from a young age, and that had helped them succeed socially.

I didn't have that same ability or that same experience.

Kapono nodded and took a sip of water.

"'I think I know where you're going," he murmured, considering me. "And if you're going in the direction that I think you are, then you're right. I found out that I would be a shifter when I was just a little kid. It was something I always knew that I would be experiencing. I grew up in Rawr County, after all. Everyone here knows. Everyone here expects and everyone here understands that being a shapeshifter is just part of life. Everyone here is a shapeshifter. And it's still something that people don't really bring to the surface except in certain circles. But still, there's an understanding here. There's a realization that this is the way we're supposed to be, and perhaps most of all, there really is an acceptance."

"And that's something I never had," I told him. I took a deep breath. No one was listening to us, but there were other people around. I lowered my voice a little. "When it happened," when I was taken, "I didn't know what to do."

"You must have been scared."

"I was," I told him, "and then I was scared to leave. I had so many chances, Kapono, but they told me I was a freak, and they told me if I tried to run away, the world would kill me. They told me nobody would want me because I was such a freak, and they made it very, very clear that they would hunt me down and destroy me if I so much as tried."

I knew too many of their secrets, after all.

People always wanted to know why someone would stay with an abuser.

That was why.

It was the fear.

I had no money when I left. I had nothing. It wasn't until I got to Honeypot and talked to Georgia that she let me know I wasn't alone and that there were other people like me. I'd had a suspicion for some time, but my access to the outside world had been very limited, and I was still young.

Those monsters had held me captive for a couple of *years*. It had been nearly five years, by my count. Five years of being put on display and being paraded around, and I had felt like a monster the entire time.

Well, I didn't feel like a monster now.

Now, I finally felt like I had some hope.

As long as Dwayne and Mike didn't figure out how to find me, I'd be okay.

As long as they didn't realize what was going on, I'd be fine.

12

Kapono

When Jim got back to town the next day, he stopped by the house for coffee before he was needed at the bar. He was working on a renovation project in the basement. His goal was to create a downstairs area with an additional bar where people could drink. He also wanted to add in things like arcade games.

I was down with the idea.

Any kind of innovation or growth was good in my mind.

The truth was that running a bar, even in a shifter town, wasn't always easy. When Jim arrived, he didn't bother knocking. He just opened the door, kicked off his shoes, and walked inside.

Darla looked up sharply from where she was sitting at the kitchen table with a cup of coffee.

"Easy," Jim said, instantly noticing that she was scared. "I'm Jim." He stopped where he was and just waited the same way you might pause when you met someone's new kitten that was a little nervous or anxious.

In some ways, Darla was like a kitten: wide-eyed, innocent. Sweet. Soft.

Fuck.

The longer this little game went on, the more I liked her, and I knew just what a bad idea it was. One of these days, I was going to realize that I was no longer *pretending* to be crazy about her and that I was, in fact, crazy about her.

Jim's idea to stand still seemed to work, though, because she immediately relaxed. I stepped beside her and placed my hand on her shoulder. Giving her a comforting squeeze, I looked up at my friend. He raised an eyebrow.

Yeah, Jim wasn't dumb.

I might have been able to trick other people with my charade, but even if Jim hadn't been in on the fact that Darla was in trouble, I didn't think he was going to buy my lie that

"Jim, this is Darla. Darla, Jim."

"Nice to meet you," Darla said. She didn't get up to meet him or shake his hand. That was okay. It certainly wasn't required in any way that she do more than wave at him. Jim certainly wasn't offended.

Some of the other shifters - mostly the wolves - were all about customs and traditions. If someone didn't get up to greet a wolf, they'd take it as a total snub, which didn't really seem fair. It wasn't a snub. It was just...

Well, it was just how life was.

"You as well. I'm sorry I wasn't here the other day," he said.

"It's totally fine."

"It's not fine," Jim said. "I know that you needed me to be there, and I wasn't. I apologize. I'm just glad that my business partner here decided to step up and help you."

"Well, he did a little more than that."

Jim cocked his head, considering what she'd just said. "What do you mean?"

Darla shot me a look. "You didn't tell him."

I hadn't.

"It's okay," I said quickly before she started to panic. I was starting to get to know Darla's little tells. A lot of things seemed to make her anxious and uncomfortable. Nervous. "I just didn't have a chance." And I didn't want to bother him while he was gone.

"What is it?"

"I told everyone we're married," I said.

Silence.

I wasn't sure what I expected, but it definitely wasn't the silence that followed. Then, just when I was about to explain myself and justify what I'd done, Jim started laughing.

"You serious?"

"Dead serious." And to be honest, I was slightly offended at the fact that he found this so funny.

"You? And you?"

"Yes," Darla nodded. "Wait, why is this funny?"

"Because people have been waiting years for this clown to get married," Jim smiled. "And I have a feeling that they're going to love you, Darla. They're just going to love you."

*

Jim and I had known each other forever. literally. He was one of the best people I'd ever met, so it was important to me that he like the woman I'd chosen to be my "wife."

Even though Jim was in on the secret, it quickly became clear that even he was thinking of Darla as my wife.

A few days after the two of them met, Jim and Kellan came over for dinner. Kellan and Darla quickly connected, talking about music and their favorite bands. Kellan loved to play guitar and Darla had always wanted to learn. They quickly connected over this and started to bond. It was kind of a cool feeling to see two people start to feel comfortable and relaxed around each other.

And I was starting to feel like there really was something special about the way that Darla interacted with the people in Rawr County.

Kellan and Darla were on the porch and Jim and I were sitting at the table drinking what had to be the best whiskey I'd ever had.

"She likes you," he said.

I looked over at him. He was watching Kellan and Darla sitting on the top step of the porch. They were leaning close together as Kellan showed her how to hold her fingers and which strings to pluck to create a melody that was perhaps the most lovely sound in the world.

I didn't care that the music wasn't perfect or that the notes she played weren't always right. I just cared that she was happy, and she was doing something.

"I like her, too," I said.

"You shouldn't let her go" Jim declared. His voice was low enough that I knew Darla and Kellan couldn't overhear. Well, Darla couldn't. She was so focused on the song that even if she'd been paying attention, she might not have noticed.

"That's not my decision to make," I said.

It wasn't.

Not really.

Darla had to make her own choices, and if what she wanted was to move on with her life, then that was what she had to do.

There would most likely come a point where she was ready to leave. There would be a time when she thought she should get out of Rawr County and go start fresh.

Right now, though, she was safe.

The people who were looking for her wouldn't find her here. Eventually, they'd get tired of searching and they'd give up, and then she'd really be free to do as she pleased.

And that could be anything.

"Don't be an idiot," Jim said to me.

"What?"

"I know what you're thinking."

"Somehow, I doubt that."

"I'm older than you," he reminded me.

"Handsomer, too," I snapped, "but what difference does that make?"

Jim blinked, staring at me. "Are you trying to insult me with compliments about my physical appearance?"

It was my turn to stare. A little. Okay, so perhaps that hadn't been the best strategy.

At least I didn't have to worry about hurting Jim's feelings, I supposed.

I was in awe of him. Even when I didn't agree with his methodology, I agreed with the fact that he really did know his stuff.

And besides, maybe he was right about mates.

Still, I wasn't quite ready to accept it just yet.

"What do you know about mates?" I asked him.

"I know a lot more than you think."

"Really? Name one thing."

"I know that you have never felt the way you feel around her."

I stared.

"And I know she makes you feel complete."

He had me there.

"And I know that no matter what you say, and no matter how big a game you're talking, you really do want what's best for her. The idea of losing herself makes you feel like you're going to throw up," he added.

And I couldn't stop myself from nodding.

Yes.

Yes, I did feel all of those things and more.

"That's because she's your mate," he said. "Trust me on this, friend. I know a mate when I see one, and that girl? She's yours."

13

Darla

The longer I stayed in Wishville, the more I started to feel safe. It was like nothing else mattered than just being there and being free. A few more days passed, but it felt like it was years. That was the thing that felt strangest to me. Everything was just so comfortable, so peaceful.

And I really did feel safe.

When was the last time I'd felt this way?

Had I ever, really?

After my parents died, I'd gone to live with my aunt, and even that hadn't felt safe. Aunt Susan had been kind. She'd given me a place to live. It was definitely a nice, comfortable house with plenty of room for a kid like me to explore and play in, but it had never felt peaceful. There had been things I wasn't supposed to touch and rooms I wasn't supposed to enter. Things like the China cabinet had always been a looming cloud that threatened to unleash hell if I touched them. It had been an anxious sort of upbringing.

There had never been a moment where I'd felt accepted or like I truly belonged.

Was that something I would ever feel?

Now, with Kapono, things were starting to look up. I spent my days running with him and my nights working in his bar. Within a couple of shifts, I had already gotten to know most of the regulars. To my surprise, they'd all readily accepted me as his "wife."

A few people had even brought us gifts, which was unexpected, but really cool. Kapono didn't want to keep any of the gifts. He told me I could have them all.

"For your place," he'd told me.

As if I was going to have a place of my own.

As if he wasn't going to try to make me stay here.

As if he didn't think I owed him anything or that I was obligated to stay.

As if I could make the choice.

One day, the two of us were running in the middle of the afternoon. That was the time I liked to run most, I'd discovered. Because Kapono ran a bar, he tended to sleep in and then spend the afternoon lounging around.

I'd started to like it, too.

But I'd found, over time, that having a little bit of time in the afternoon felt good. I'd found that having some time to myself could be really, really relaxing.

Most of the time, Kapono and I ran together, but some afternoons, he'd sprawl out in the yard, and I'd go off on my own.

Today was one of those days.

I left him sleeping in his tiger form in the yard. Then I raced out toward the mountains, running through these vast, open fields near his house. Nobody was around. Nobody was here to see me. Nobody was going to be bothered by the fact that there was a real-life wild tiger out here.

I ran for an hour or two, just racing until I reached a cool, relaxing place surrounded by trees and a little waterfall.

There I sat by the edge of the little pool, and I just closed my eyes.

This was it.

This was what I wanted.

I wanted to be safe.

More than anything else in the world, I wanted the peace that came with being here.

I never wanted to leave.

14

Kapono

The bar was busier than usual. For a Wednesday night, the crowd was steady. That was always the goal, and it was something I liked to see. While most bars knew they'd be busy on Fridays and Saturdays, I wanted our little slice of paradise to grow and expand. Forward motion was something that Jim and I talked about a lot, but it was often easy to talk about it. It was harder to actually make it happen.

The two of us had a lot of ideas for growing and expanding, starting with the expansion of the bar itself. Once we had the basement open, it was going to be a lot easier for us to host themed parties and special events just because we'd have more space. Besides, I was looking forward to the total vibe we'd have.

I'd always love bars that were creative and comfortable. Having a place where people could throw back some beers and enjoy things like playing old games felt like heaven to me.

"Did you have fun this afternoon?" I asked Darla, teasing her a little bit as I made a drink for one of our patrons. She smirked and nodded. She was a lot of fun. If I'd known having a pretend wife was going to be this cool, I would have done it years ago.

"Yeah, she said. I had a good time."

That morning, the two of us had made love in the shower before going on a run that lasted hours. I'd taken her up against a tree and again by a waterfall. It was fun and relaxing and freeing. There was something so damn wonderful about being with her that it really made me feel like my whole heart was exploding.

She was lovely, and she was learning that there was more to life than being afraid.

When she'd first arrived, Darla had been scared constantly, but now, only weeks later, she was starting to feel a little more relaxed, and she was starting to feel like she had a place.

My only concern was that one day, she'd decide that she was ready to move on from this place and I'd have to say goodbye to her. I'd have to actually walk away and I didn't want to.

I wanted her to stay.

It was kind of a scary thought, but it was one I would have to come to terms with eventually.

"And tonight?" I asked her, glancing back over. "How's your night going?"

"Tonight's been busy, but good. I think I'm finally getting the hang of this waitress thing."

"She's good at it," came a familiar voice. "You should give her a raise."

I wasn't really sure what the policy was on giving raises to pretend spouses, but I made a mental note to ask Jim about it. Then I realized who was talking.

"Cosmo?" I asked, looking up at the dragon shifter. He smiled. Cosmo showed a little too much teeth when he smiled - one of the many indicators that he was, in fact, a dragon shifter.

Unlike cats, who liked to lay around and relax, Cosmo was always ready for action. If it was up to him, he'd probably be holed up in a penthouse somewhere surrounded by money, but he wasn't. He worked for a living, although there was a part of me that assumed it was mostly because he liked one of his assistants.

She was pretty, and he was all man.

"The one and only," Cosmo nodded. He was wearing a suit to the bar, which was strange, too. Who wore a suit to a bar? Especially a place like this. I held back from rolling my eyes, but only barely.

"Your name is Cosmo?" Darla asked.

He nodded.

"And you're drinking cosmos? Isn't that a little on the nose?"

He frowned at her.

"I'm sorry. I ordered a drink. I didn't order judgment to go along with it."

Darla laughed and turned back to me. She tapped her fingers on the bar as she waited. I was moving as quickly as I could, and when I turned back around, I held up the glass.

"Is this one for him?" I asked. She nodded.

"He was sitting at a table when I came up to order it for him."

"I figured I'd move," Cosmo said, reaching for the glass. "Save you a bit of walking time. Besides, it's always good to talk to an old friend. There wasn't any room at the bar when I first arrived," he informed me.

"We're busy tonight." I wasn't sure why. It wasn't our usual vibe. Our goal with this place was to keep things as calm and mellow as possible, but sometimes the crowds got bigger than we expected.

"That's okay," Cosmo said. "Congrats on all the business."

I nodded and turned to start making another drink. People were starting to line up at the bar, which unfortunately meant that I wasn't going to have as much time to talk to Cosmo as I wanted to, but that was okay.

I made a mental note to call the dragon shifter the next day, and I kept making drinks.

*

The next night, business was at a much more usual pace. Thursday nights were never super crowded. We didn't do Thirsty Thursdays like some bars. This was mostly because I didn't think we'd be able to handle a crazy influx of customers before the weekend started.

I was happy about that when Cosmo came in. He wasn't alone, and he took his companion to one of the tables toward the back of the bar close to the darts and pool tables.

"Who's he with?" Darla asked, leaning against the bar. She looked over at him. In a minute, I'd go see what he wanted to drink. Even though Darla was my waitress on duty, I wanted to talk to Cosmo.

"No idea."

"Could be a girlfriend."

"Or a client."

"Client?"

"He's a lawyer," I told her. "I'm honestly surprised he didn't tell you last night. He loves to talk about it."

"Really?"

"All lawyers do."

"Is that a fact?"

I nodded. The thing about lawyers was that they were smart as hell, but they knew it. That was problematic because when someone *knew* they were smart, they were insufferable. Dragon shifters were already bad enough as it was.

"Can you get more ice?" I asked her. "I'm going to go see what he wants to drink."

Darla gave me a confused look, but she nodded and took off. I headed over to Cosmo's table to see him looking agitated and tired. Okay, so this wasn't the woman he was interested in. This was someone else. A client. Definitely a client.

"Good evening," I said.

"Shit." Cosmo closed his eyes and started rubbing his temple. "It's you."

"You're in my bar, man. What did you expect?"

"I don't know," he groaned.

"Can I get you a drink?"

The woman he was with looked from me to Cosmo and back again. She frowned before looking back at me. "I'd like a drink. Vodka tonic, please."

"Same," Cosmo said. "And bring me a couple of shots, too."

"Long day?" I asked.

"It's about to get longer."

"Is it?" I looked over at the woman.

"That's my fault, I'm afraid," she cringed. "I brought Cosmo a few contracts to look over for me. He's doing it as a favor and I'm afraid they're pretty annoying."

"That's an understatement," he said. "Drinks are on Jennifer's tab tonight."

I looked at the woman for confirmation and she nodded. "That's fine. Actually, I'll take two drinks, too."

"Coming right up," I chuckled, and turned to head back to the bar.

Darla was there leaning against the counter when I came over. Instead of starting to pour the drinks, I dragged her and kissed her.

"Hey, kitty cat," I purred in her ear. She laughed and grabbed me, pulling me close.

"Hey."

"It's going to be a good night."

"It always is with you."

If I didn't know better, I'd say that she was into me. I was definitely into her. I was definitely so totally into her. I didn't think that I was supposed to be. It certainly didn't feel like it was right.

I was, though.

And I knew that this was going to explode at some point. There was no way a cat like me was deserving of someone like her. She was a tigress. A goddess. She deserved everything the world had to offer and more.

When Darla decided that she was ready to move on, when she decided that she was safe, then I would be there for her. I would support her decision.

But I knew without a doubt that it was going to be very, very painful for me.

I knew that it was going to hurt.

And as I kissed her, I knew that I was going to regret losing her the moment that she left.

15

Darla

Cosmo was an interesting person, but then again, so was the person that he was with in the bar. I was starting to be able to tell who was a shapeshifter and who wasn't. I still couldn't do things like "scent out" what kind of shifter they were, but from what I could tell, that wasn't an uncommon problem to have.

I brought them refills on their drinks, and as I set down the beverages on their table, they both looked up at me. They weren't together. They definitely weren't interested in each other. They did, however, both seem very interested in me.

Not in a sexual way, of course, but in a way that just screamed curiosity.

"So, Mrs. Kapono," Cosmo said before I could slip away quietly. "How was the honeymoon?"

Honeymoon?

Shit.

Kapono and I had tried to cover all of our bases and we'd *tried* to think of everything we'd possibly need to think about in order to make our story convincing, but we hadn't thought about what we had done for a honeymoon - or if we had.

"Oh," I said, straining to keep my face neutral. "Well, you know, there will be time for that later."

The woman with Cosmo looked up at me. "When? He works all the time."

"Good question, Jennifer. I was thinking the same thing."

"That's what I thought," Cosmo sneered."

"What you thought?"

"You aren't actually married."

I paled.

How could he have guessed that?

"What? Yes, we are. We're in love," I doubled down, jutting my chin out. If Cosmo wanted to be like that, he could be like that, but I wasn't going to let him be like that on my time. I didn't want to be insulted or bothered. didn't want to be annoyed or irritated in this way.

For a moment, I thought Jennifer was going to take my side, but then, after a minute, she started to nod.

"He's right," she said. "Why is he right?"

"Hey!" It was Cosmo's turn to look annoyed. "I'm allowed to be right sometimes."

Jennifer rolled her eyes. "If it was up to you, you'd be right all of the time."

"There's nothing wrong with taking pride in what I do."

Being right isn't something you should be taking pride in."

"Why not? Being nice is wonderful."

I stared at them both.

"You aren't right," I said again. I wasn't sure if he had liquid courage from all of the alcohol or if I was just anxious and tired from working all night, but I was starting to feel a little worn down.

Up until this point, everyone had just accepted that Kapono and I were, in fact, married. It had been a bit unnerving, actually. I wasn't sure how people were so certain that we were married after just being told it a single time. What I'd gathered was that

Kapono was spontaneous and surprising. This meant that no matter what he did, people were always caught off guard by it.

Now, his "decision" to get married was just as random and unexpected for people.

I wasn't really sure how I felt about that.

"Shut up."

"I'm definitely right."

"Not at all."

"Oh, I think that I am."

"No."

Cosmo leaned back in his seat and stared at me. The high top stools had backs on them, but I still half expected him to fall off the stool.

"You aren't married to Kapono."

Cosmo was insistent, and it was actually kind of annoying.

How dare he?

How dare he make such an accusation?

It was true, of course. It was true that the two of us weren't actually married, but that wasn't the thing that bothered me. The thing that bothered me most was that he'd seen through the charade. He'd figured it out somehow.

He's seen through *everything*.

I had to keep lying to him, though. I couldn't let him know that something was amiss because if he did, he'd definitely have something to say about it. This wasn't the kind of guy who was going to let things go.

That was probably part of the reason he was such a good lawyer. I had a feeling that Cosmo was like a dog with a bone. If he got something in his head, if he got his mind set to it, then he'd never stop wondering.

This was going to be a real problem for me.

And I hated that.

"It's okay," Jennifer spoke up. She turned to Cosmo. "Can't you see that she doesn't want to talk about it?"

"Oh, I can see," he nodded. "I just don't know why. What are you hiding, tiger?"

I paled as I stared at him. All of a sudden, I felt like I was going to be sick. He knew, I thought. He knew that something was going on, knew that something was up, and I was going to be absolutely sick about it.

I didn't want to start running again just yet. Not when I'd just started to get settled.

Eventually, I was going to have to run. I knew that. Being here indefinitely wasn't really an option. At some point, I was going to have to say goodbye to Kapono, say goodbye to the lessons he'd taught me, and I'd have to move on.

Then again, maybe that wasn't really fair.

The reality was that I didn't have to say goodbye to what he'd taught me.

Those were lessons I could take with me for a very long time. I could take all of the things I'd learned and I could apply them to my future no matter what came next.

I just didn't know what "next" looked like. Not just yet.

"Nothing," I blurted out, even though I was pretty sure I'd made things about ten times worse with my overreaction.

I'd panicked.

I would be the first to admit that.

I was saved from having to talk anymore because someone called my name and I turned away, desperately ready to go help someone else with their questions and problems. I could get drink orders or maybe answer questions about how the ka basement project was coming along. I had an endless number of options. I just knew that I didn't want to be anywhere near Cosmo or his nosy dragon face.

16

Kapono

Something had spooked her. I couldn't say for certain what it was. All I knew was that all of a sudden, she was afraid. I couldn't tell at first, but as Darla darted away from Cosmo's table and started making her way toward a couple of patrons who were eagerly ready to order drinks, I could smell her anxiety.

I made my way over to her and began working alongside her. I didn't want to alert anyone just yet that she might have been afraid or upset. Nobody needed to know that. Nobody needed to know that she had gotten worked up while at the office. I didn't want her to feel bad.

And oh, I didn't want her to be afraid.

That was the thing I worried about the most. I didn't want my sweet girl to feel scared. She'd been afraid and alone for so very long that now, now I wanted her to feel nothing but utter safety and total security.

The first chance I had to pull her away, I guided her to the bar. She handed me a list of drink orders and I accepted it, but I didn't make a move to start making drinks. Instead, I just *looked* at her. She was tired. She reeked of anxiety.

"Are you okay?"

"I'm fine."

"No, you're not fine."

"I'm okay."

She was insistent, but I knew it was a lie. Everything that was coming out of her mouth was a total lie. I found myself filled with the urge to grab her and kiss her hot lying mouth until she forgot about being anything but honest, but I didn't.

Instead, I glanced over at Cosmo, who was staring at me. I didn't like it when he did that. Cosmo had very beady, sneering eyes. I didn't like how he just stared at people all of the time. It was actually kind of annoying, especially considering how right now, emotions were high. I was trying to figure out what was wrong with Darla, but I knew that the answers were with Cosmo.

Instead of pressing her right there in the bar, I made a mental note to bug her later. Right now, I'd go talk to Cosmo about it and see what the dragon shifter was willing to tell me. He was good at keeping secrets, but he was also kind of a blabbermouth when he wanted to be. Chances were that if he'd said anything annoying or mean to my girl, he'd be willing to say it to me, too.

I made my way over to his table. He was sitting with a woman I didn't know. She'd been in the bar a few times, but always alone, and she was always very hesitant to talk.

She looked up at me as I approached.

"I'm Kapono," I said by way of introduction. The woman looked sweet: much too sweet to be hanging out with someone like Cosmo. The dragon shifter was something of a notorious grumpy pants.

"Jennifer," she said

"Are you having a good time tonight?"

"It's a work meeting, "Cosmo explained. "None of us is having a good time tonight. "What do you expect?"

"Better manners," I shrugged.

He glared. For just a second, his eyes changed colors. I really hated when dragons did that. His eyes morphed into this bright yellow color before turning back to normal. I half-expected him to shift into his dragon form right then, but was thrilled when he didn't.

Apparently, Jennifer had the same feeling I did because she wrinkled her nose as she frowned at Cosmo.

"You know what?" Jennifer stood up. "I think I'm good on tonight. Thanks for your help, Cosmo." She smoothed her skirt and reached for her tiny black purse. She started to step away, but Cosmo wasn't going to let her off the hook that easily.

"Don't forget to close your tab," Cosmo held up his glass. "You're buying remember?" The dragon was insistent. I had to give him that. Cosmo was *not* the kind of guy who let anything go. If "obsession" was something you could get paid for, he'd have his own business. I supposed being a lawyer was the next best thing. He literally got paid to obsess over little details. It was kind of annoying, actually.

Jennifer glared at him. For just a second, I thought she was going to say something shitty, but she didn't. Instead, she just nodded. I was impressed. As it turned out, she was a woman of her word and she wasn't going to let anything slide by her. She turned and walked toward the bar. Cosmo's eyes didn't follow her. Not even a little.

So, he wasn't interested in her.

It wasn't a romantic kind of meeting, was it?

Apparently, it really had been a work thing, but why they'd meet in a bar, I didn't know, and why they'd meet without anyone else, I also didn't know.

"What kind of meeting was that?" I asked, gesturing to the table.

"Fuck you," Cosmo glared. "None of your business." He crossed his arms and looked like a petulant, whiny little boy.

I shrugged.

"You share with me, I share with you," I offered.

Cosmo knew the game.

He *knew* how being a shifter worked.

He also knew that I wasn't playing. I wasn't going to give him what he wanted if he didn't give me what I wanted, and what I wanted was information. What I *wanted* were answers.

"You have to share if you want me to share," I reminded him.

His eyes, which were still just as beady looking as before, narrowed.

"I know how the world works," he said.

"Then start acting like it."

"You always have to be right. Has anyone ever told you that?"

"As a matter of fact, my mother tells me that every chance she gets," I informed him. It was one of the things the two of us had fought about endlessly, especially in my childhood. My mother was the kind of person who seemed to think that any sort of irritation or annoyance on her part was enough to make me change.

It hadn't been.

The two of us still fought to this day, although we'd gotten much better over the years. These days, she was more supportive than bickering. I had the feeling that with age, she'd gotten tired of fighting and arguing. Over time, the idea of yelling at me or trying to be "right" had worn her out. She was done with all of that.

It had been quite delightful that she'd enjoyed meeting Darla so much. The irritation my mom often felt seemed to be fading even more these days. Besides, now that she was busy planning a reception – at my expense, of course – she was even more content.

Cosmo sighed.

"What has gotten into you, man?" I asked him. Cosmo had always been someone I'd been able to count on. He'd always been really cool and calm and relaxed. He'd just been fun.

These days, though, he was kind of a prick. It felt like anytime I said anything to Cosmo, he just got mad. He was constantly irritable, and he viewed every comment anyone made as some sort of offensive remark even when it wasn't intended to be.

If I didn't know better, I would have said that Cosmo had gotten dumped.

Only, he hadn't.

The dragon shifter was notorious - no, legendary - for his "I'm single" stance. Despite the fact that he was a very, very eligible bachelor, he never seemed to find any interest in *actually* getting married. That was really one of the things that kept people so curious about him.

He was handsome, I knew, and people really liked that about him.

"Nothing."

"Liar."

"Eat me."

"You're not my type."

That got a little smirk. He shook his head. Cosmo wasn't picky about who he slept with. He didn't *date*, but he slept around when he felt like it. I wasn't sure if that was a good thing or not. Now that I had Darla, there was a part of me that wondered if I'd ever want to sleep with anyone else.

Maybe I would, but there was just something so deliciously delightful about her.

And I had a feeling that whatever happened next, Darla was going to be it for me.

It wasn't just that we'd lied about our marriage that was troubling me now...it was that I wanted it to be true.

And I had a feeling that people like Cosmo and Jim could see right through my lies.

17

Darla

Dwayne and Mike hadn't found me.

It had been days.

It had been weeks.

It had been so long that I was getting really, really comfortable and I almost - almost - believed that I was actually married to Kapono.

I wasn't, but I almost believed it.

One night, the two of us were lying in the grass outside of his house. I was in my tiger form, lying on my side. He was in his human form, leaning against me. He was singing songs about being a tiger and I was...

Well, I was wondering what I'd ever done to deserve someone like him.

"I like having you around," he said, suddenly stopping the song.

I like having you around, too.

I thought the words since I couldn't speak them, but that was it.

That was the deepest the two of us ever got when it came to conversation. We both had this understanding that one day, I was going to have to leave. One day, there would be a time, a moment, when I had to go away. I'd have to go off and do normal things and live a regular life, but I really, really didn't want to.

What I wanted was to be his.

I wanted to be so *fucking* his.

I shifted back suddenly, unpredictably, and he moved away as I changed back into my woman form. He was always giving me space, always very conscious of making sure I didn't feel too crowded or nervous.

This time, he didn't need to be nervous. This time, I was ready for him.

And I'd realized something during my time here in Rawr County. I'd learned that I really wasn't as alone as I'd always thought that I was. My captors had always tried to make me feel alone, and they'd succeeded in doing that for a very long time. They'd let me know just how isolated and broken I was.

And then Kapono had come into my life.

He was like a tornado wreaking havoc on my plans for my future. I'd come here to hide out, but I hadn't expected to fall in love. Hadn't expected to find myself thinking of him during all of my spare time.

He'd done more than just offer me a backstory and a job and a place to stay.

He'd offered me passion.

He'd offered me love.

I wasn't sure if these were things I'd ever be able to repay him for. The most wonderful thing about Kapono was that his kindness didn't seem to have an end. It was like his generosity and his sweetness knew no bounds, and that made everything even sweeter.

Even more wonderful.

"I like you, Kapono," I whispered.

The words caught in my throat because they were so hard for me to say. There was still a part of me that worried he might reject me, but he didn't. Instead, a grin slid over his face as realization dawned on him.

And then he was on me.

The two of us hadn't seemed to figure out that the "honeymoon period" usually didn't have a strict end date. Most people tried to stretch it out for ages, and there was a part of me that wanted that, too.

I hadn't set an end date, but I could feel it edging up on me. It was sneaking up, crawling toward me, and I didn't really think there was anything I could do to stop it.

At some point, I'd have to say goodbye to him.

Our time together would come to an end.

I just really, really didn't want that time to be today.

He kissed me, pushing me back in the grass. I wrapped my arms and legs around him and before he'd even started touching my breasts, he was inside of me. Like that. And I was ready for him because I wanted him.

I always wanted him.

I groaned as he filled me, thick and needy. He thrust deep inside of me and I trailed my fingers down his sides until I gripped his ass, pulling him deeper. *Needing* him deeper.

"Kapono."

I whispered his name like it was a damn promise.

Because to me, he was promising everything.

He was promising me a chance.

He was promising me a future.

He was offering me this understanding that I could do things on my own. Before I'd come to stay with Kapono, I'd really and truly believed that my entire world was messy. I'd thought that my future was nonexistent. I had thought, above all else, that whatever came next was going to be painful.

Being with him, though, was anything but.

It was incredible.

And I was starting to fall for him.

I hated it, on some level, because I knew that it was going to run its course. Everything good always came to an end at some point, but right now, I just wanted to feel him. I just wanted to be with him.

And I wanted to give him some good memories of me before everything came crashing down.

Pushing him back, I climbed on top of him, straddling him.

"You're so fucking beautiful." Kapono grabbed my breasts, bouncing them as I rode him. I found myself grinding down on him, enjoying everything about the way that he felt. It was like nothing else mattered, like nothing else was going to ever come between the two of us because what we had was incredible.

Perfect.

Magical.

We came together, a mixture of happiness and ecstasy beneath the starry sky, and then I collapsed on him and pressed kisses to his cheeks.

I could have stayed there with him forever.

But every good thing had to come to an end, and I knew that our time was almost up.

18

Kapono

It was a Tuesday afternoon when the man stopped in the bar. He wasn't from Rawr County. That much was obvious. This guy was tall, but he wasn't muscular the way shifters usually were. He was scrawny and lean, but not like a wolf.

Like a spider.

No, not like a spider.

Like a human.

This man was no shifter.

If this guy was in Rawr County, then there was a reason, but it wasn't anything good. He looked around the bar, but not the way someone who was looking for a good table would do. Instead, he seemed methodical. He wasn't *looking*. He was *searching*.

Could this be the guy who was after Darla?

Could this be the asshole?

He caught my eye and lifted a hand.

"Howdy," he called out, waltzing toward the counter like he owned the place. He hooked a thumb into his too-tight jeans. His cowboy boots were out of place. They were polished, for one thing. They didn't have a speck of dirt on them, for another.

Who was this clown?

And why was he trying to look country?

He wasn't. I'd bet my ass he'd never even set foot outside of a city before. Whatever he was up to, it was something bad.

And he *reeked* of anger.

I'd run my bar long enough that I'd had my share of humans in here. It was just that most of the time, they weren't pretending to be something that they weren't. They weren't *pretending* to be in charge of the situation. They weren't acting like they were in control.

This guy was.

Whoever he was, he was used to having people bend to him and listen to what he had to say.

Maybe he wasn't the one who was after my "wife."

Maybe he was just some dickwad from another city who was stopping through for a drink.

"What can I do for you?" I kept my voice even and flat. I didn't want him to feel welcome here. Didn't want him to think he was going to be offered anything special. I was glad as hell that Darla was out exploring the mountains as a tiger. She'd gone out with Jim and his husband and the three of them were planning to get back before the bar officially opened for the night at five. It was four now, so I wasn't sure why this dude was wandering in.

"Can I get a drink?"

"Not open yet."

"Aw, come on." He smiled in a way that said he'd done this many times before. He didn't seem to care even slightly that he was inconveniencing me in any way. Instead, he just shrugged and smirked like this was the easiest thing to understand in the world.

"Sorry. We open in an hour. You can come back then."

My phone vibrated in my pocket, but I ignored it. I turned away from the man and set down the glass I'd been drying.

Turning back around, I grabbed another wet glass and continued drying it. Then I jerked my head toward the door and hoped the guy would take a hint.

Anger flashed in his eyes, but only for a second. If I hadn't been staring at him, I would have completely missed it. Instead of leaving, he flatted his lips together and then gave me a tight, short nod. He cocked his head.

"I'm looking for someone."

"There are no strip clubs here," I said, intentionally misunderstanding what he was saying. He glared at me.

"That's not what I mean."

"Oh? What do you mean?"

"I'm looking for someone."

It was him.

It was the man who wanted Darla.

Suddenly, it was just very obvious to me, and it took every ounce of strength in me not to throw him out of the bar on his ass.

"Afraid I can't help you," I shrugged. "I don't know too many people."

The man stared at me.

"She's a girl. New in town. Mid-twenties."

I shrugged and turned to the register. I started fiddling with it, pretending that it was broken, and I had to fix it.

"You got a name for this girl?" I asked him. Maybe there was a chance that it wasn't her.

Maybe.

"She uses a few different names," he said. "Lately, she's been going by something with a D." He started snapping his fingers, trying to pretend like he didn't know. "Daffodil, Diana...oh, no, I remember. Darla."

I looked up at him.

Was this him?

Was this the man who had caused all of the problems for my sweet fake-wife?

My eyes narrowed.

"Who?"

"Darla," he said. He spoke a bit more confidently that time, and I knew.

I knew that her days of hiding were about to come to an end. We'd have to take steps to protect her now. I'd have to chase this asshole out of town and hoped he never came back, or I'd have to take care of him myself.

He wasn't a shifter. That much was obvious. He reeked of humanity, so I knew that whatever happened next, it was going to be me versus him.

Well, and possibly his accomplice, whom I assumed was also human.

Before I could make a decision as to what I needed to do, my phone rang. It was on the back counter, and I turned when I heard the sound. I grabbed it and shoved it in my pocket, but when I turned back around, he was gone.

The man had left.

And I hadn't caught him.

Leaping over the bar, I ran to the front door and tugged it open, but all that I saw was a car speeding off down the road.

I'd missed him.

Well, shit.

19

Darla

He was standing in the kitchen making dinner, and I was seated at the wide oak kitchen table. there was a spider plant at the center of the table that Sloan had given me. Apparently, when she wasn't bartending, she was working on her green thumb. It was kind of cool, actually. How often did you meet someone who just wanted to give you plants?

Kapono had been acting weird all night. When we'd been at the bar the night before, he'd been anxious and uncomfortable. Even Jim had noticed. He'd asked me what was going on with Kapono, but I didn't know.

I still didn't know why.

All day long, he'd been anxious. He'd been going to the windows a lot and checking his phone. When I'd invited him to go run with me, he'd not only turned me down, but asked me not to go because he thought we should stay home today.

It was weird.

Nobody had found me.

Nobody had located me, so I wasn't in any sort of danger.

There *had* to be another reason that he was acting so out of character.

Had he found someone new?

Was that it?

Maybe he'd met someone new and he wanted to get into a relationship with *them*. Perhaps he'd just decided that enough was enough. I wasn't sure. All I knew was that he was going to be the death of me. He was going to completely destroy me if I wasn't careful.

So, I had to be careful.

We'd spent the whole day relaxing, albeit separately. He'd been at the house, and I'd gone on a long walk to clear my mind.

I think there was a part of me that knew.

There was a part of me that understood it was time.

Still, I had to ask him. What if I had it all wrong?

What if I wasn't reading this situation correctly?

I'd spent years feeling like everything I was doing was wrong. With Dwayne and Mike, I'd always gotten it wrong. No matter what I did, I was incorrect, and that had been a very painful thing for me to experience.

They'd been cruel to me, yet they'd played the roles of good magicians when we were on stage. Most people didn't know I was a shapeshifter. They just thought me changing into a tiger was part of the act. The people who did know didn't think anything was wrong. They didn't know I wasn't allowed to leave. They didn't know I wasn't even being paid.

Even the other people who worked the show with us – venue directors, organizers, and sometimes other magicians – didn't realize just how dire my situation was.

That was the thing about being abused: from the outside, things almost always looked normal.

Right now, my relationship with Kapono looked normal.

Only, it wasn't.

I could tell that something was wrong.

I just didn't know what it was.

"Kapono?" I asked, looking over at him. He looked up sharply at me. A smile flitted across his face but disappeared almost as quickly. If I'd blinked, I would have missed it. Now his eyes held sadness and irritation. Frustration, perhaps.

If he wanted to get rid of me, I needed to just get him to tell me. I needed to just rip off the proverbial bandage. I knew that much. If I didn't get the guts to face him, I'd always wonder.

"What is it?"

"Is something wrong?"

He stopped what he was doing and turned to me.

"Wrong?"

I nodded.

There had to be something, right? Like, there had to be a reason that he'd been so strange and weird since he'd gotten home. I didn't know what it was, though.

The reality was that he didn't have to tell me everything. He was under no obligation to tell me if he'd had a bad day or a good day or something in-between.

"Nothing's wrong," he said.

I nodded, turning back toward the snack I'd prepared. The apple slices and peanut butter should have been delicious, but suddenly, my appetite was gone.

"My mistake," I found myself sliding down the chair a little. I didn't want to get into a fight, but I also didn't want to make it seem like I was forcing him to talk to me.

Kapono had been on his own for a long time. He didn't have to share anything with me. It would be nice, yes, but it definitely wasn't required.

He was his own person.

He could do as he pleased.

"What are you talking about?"

"It's nothing," I said.

He came over and pulled out the chair beside me. Then he sat down, too. He placed his hands on mine. His eyes slid to the apples for just a second.

"Not going to eat them?"

"I'm not hungry anymore."

He watched me for a minute, and then he sighed. His ran a hand through his hair before placing it on my shoulder. Then he just *looked* at me.

"It's something," he said. "It's not nothing."

My stomach twisted. This was it. This was the moment where I found out if I had a future with Kapono or not. This was the moment where I found out if the two of us were going to have a wonderful adventure...

Or not.

"What?" I asked him. I took a deep breath. I could handle this. Whatever it was, I could handle it. Maybe Kapono would say that he no longer wanted to be with me. If that was the case, then I'd be okay. I was a big girl. I'd been dumped before. I could deal with this. I could deal with all of it.

"Someone came into the bar," he told me.

Instantly, I felt cold. It was like there was ice wrapping around me, like I was suddenly freezing in place.

"Someone?" I asked quietly.

Of course, I knew who he meant.

Of course, it had to be *him*.

It was Dwayne. I knew it instantly. Dwayne was always the smooth talker. He'd always been the one who was in charge of getting things done. Mike was the one who was mean and malicious.

Together, they were unstoppable. Their magic act had always been subpar until they'd gotten me. That was when they'd started making regular money with their performances.

Oh, they mostly traveled around and performed in small venues. It was nothing really to write home about, but that hadn't stopped either of them from being stupidly proud or ridiculously happy for themselves.

And it had left me hurt.

Broken.

Afraid.

For years, I'd fantasized about having someone just swoop in and save me, and that day had finally come.

Only, I'd had to run to him.

I'd had to be brave first.

But Kapono had been here, waiting with open arms.

"How did they find me?" I asked.

I'd been so careful. I had been cautious and I'd watched my back. I'd kept my head down. Honestly, I didn't really do a lot unless it was with Kapono at the bar.

"I have no idea," he said, "but I'm going to keep you safe."

Only, he couldn't.

He couldn't protect me from this, I realized, and worse than that, I couldn't protect him.

What if Mike and Dwayne realized just how important Kapono had become to me? I hadn't been gone very long, but of course they'd want to hunt me down. I was their prized show pony, after all. They weren't going to just let me go.

I knew what I needed to do, but I also didn't know if I actually had the guts.

Could I leave him now?

After all of this?

Could I leave Kapono before they found him?

20

Kapono

I could tell the second she started thinking of leaving, and I had to crush that right away. That wasn't going to happen. I wasn't going to let Darla be some sacrificial lamb. I needed her too much. I was far too crazy about her.

And I'd become addicted to her.

It hadn't taken very long. Maybe the stories were right, and she really was my mate because I couldn't imagine living without her. It had only been a few weeks since she'd come to Rawr County, but it felt like I'd known her for years.

Shaking my head, I reached for her cheek and touched it softly. My sweet, beautiful mate was scared. She was sad. Worried. Nervous.

But she was safe here.

I wasn't going to let them hurt her. I wasn't going to let anyone hurt her ever again.

"No," I said firmly. She blinked, looking up at me.

"What?"

"You aren't going anywhere."

"Kapono..." Darla's voice trailed off and she looked up at me. She shook her head. Her bright eyes closed for just a moment. She took a deep breath and when she opened them again, I could see the resolve there.

"You aren't going anywhere," I repeated.

I'd say it again.

And again.

I'd do whatever it took to keep her here.

"I'll tie you to the bed," I threatened a little playfully. "I'll fuck you silly until you're too tired to try to run away."

It wasn't much of a threat, but she started to tear up. Ignoring my joke, she whispered to me.

"We don't really have a choice."

Only, we did. We did have a choice. We had a lot of choices. We had the choice to stay together and stick this out.

What was the worst thing these guys were going to do?

Yell at me?

Try to fight me?

I was a fucking tiger. They weren't going to be able to touch me. No matter what happened, they were going to be useless against me.

There was no way they'd be able to get me.

No matter what happened, I was going to be just fine, and so was she.

I'd come to the point where I realized that there were few things in life that I really wanted. I wanted to see my friend succeed and I wanted our bar to do well, but those were just things that would be *nice*.

What I wanted, what I really wanted, was to protect her.

And I wanted her to be happy.

My cell rang and I growled in irritation, but I reached for it anyway. Jim was calling, and I couldn't leave him hanging. His mother was still sick, and if he needed to go be with her, then he was going to need me to cover him at the bar.

"This isn't over," I told Darla firmly. "Don't leave." I have expected she was going to bolt as soon as I answered the call.

She nodded, but her hands were gripping the table, and I knew that if I even thought about leaving the room or turning my back, she was going to try to run. She'd done it before escaping these guys, and she'd do it again if she had to. That was just the world we lived in.

Instead of moving away to take the call, I stayed where I was. I held her hand tightly and hoped that it was a comforting gesture: not a scary one.

"Jim. You okay?"

"It's my mom," he said. His voice fell, and I knew that this wasn't going to be a simple call. "She's gone."

Shit.

"Jim..."

My heart broke for my friend. I knew that he'd been trying to keep it together. He'd been at the bar quite a bit, but he'd been spreading his time between the hospital and the basement where he was still working on expanding the bar.

"It's okay," he said quietly. "I know she was ready."

That might have been true. Maybe *she* was ready, but that didn't mean that Jim was ready. That was the problem with death, wasn't it? Sometimes the people who were left behind were the ones who struggled. Someone was leaving the world, but it felt like they were abandoning the people who didn't get to come along for the journey.

"I'll come right over," I told him.

"No," Jim said. "I'm with Kellan. We're going to go take care of a few things."

"Can I do anything for you?" Jim really was like a brother to me. Nobody could ever replace Grant, and I knew Jim would never want to try, but he'd *always* been there for me.

"I'll let you know," Jim said. "For now, can you cover me at One More Howl?"

"You know I can," I told him. "I'll do whatever you need. Just take your time, okay? There's no need to rush back."

Grief could take time to work through, and losing his mom wasn't something that my friend was going to just "get over" in a day or two.

He'd need time, and I was happy to let him take it.

When I got off the phone, I set my cell face-down on the table. There would be no more distractions. Then I walked to where Darla was sitting, and I reached for her. Pulling the street woman to her feet, I kissed her.

"Kapono..."

"Jim's going to be gone for a few days," I told her.

"I heard. I'm sorry about his mom."

"She lived a good life," I offered.

"That doesn't really make it easier to say goodbye, does it?"

Not for me, no. Knowing that someone had lived a good, wonderful, relaxing life had never been enough to make me feel happy about things ending like this.

"Not so much," I admitted.

"You're going to ask me to stay. Aren't you?"

I was.

I was going to ask her to stay.

And some of it was selfish, sure, but some of it wasn't. Darla wanted to run away, but I needed her here. I needed her to be with me.

And I *wanted* her to be with me.

I nodded slowly.

"Kapono, you don't know these guys."

"I know their type."

"They're different..."

"Darla, I will not let them hurt you again."

"But-"

"No," I interrupted her, shaking my head. I tilted her chin up toward me. "I will *not* let them hurt you again."

"Kapono, they captured me. I thought they were going to help me learn to control my shifter powers, but they exploited it instead. Dwayne fancies himself a magician. Not a magic user, but like..." She shook her head. "Like, he did magic shows. And I was part of the act." She closed her eyes and took a deep breath. "I had so many chances to run and I didn't. I was so scared. All of the time, I was afraid."

Rage started pulsing through my veins as I realized the extent of what these men had done to Darla. Not only had they taken her freedom, but they had taken her independence. They had done their best to take her identity, as well, and that was something I just didn't think I could deal with again.

It was something I didn't want *her* to have to deal with ever again.

These assholes had humiliated her. They'd taken what was supposed to be an incredible gift – being able to shapeshift –

and they'd twisted it. Contorted it. They'd taken her home and her passion and they'd just screwed with her.

"They aren't going to hurt you again," I told her.

It was a promise.

A vow.

No matter what they did, I wouldn't let them touch her.

"You can't promise that," Darla said.

"I can, and I will."

"Kapono, they're going to come back. I don't know how they found me here, but they found me, and they're going to come back."

And when they did, I'd be ready.

21

Darla

I hated that he had convinced me to stay, but he had.

It was my own problem, really, and in some ways, it was such a unique one to have. Kapono was falling in love with me, and I was falling in love with him. The whole county thought the two of us were already married, so nobody realized what was going on except for us and possibly Jim.

A few days passed and nothing happened. Jim and Kellan were handling funeral arrangements for Jim's mom, Sloan was working as usual, and Brock the bouncer had been alerted to let Kapono know about anything weird or unusual that happened.

Dwayne and Mike didn't reappear at the bar, and I knew that Kapono was starting to calm down about this, but it was premature.

They were going to *know*.

I still didn't know how.

Kapono had been guarding me for the last few days. In between lovemaking and racing around in our tiger forms, he'd never wandered too far from me. Unlike when I'd been with Dwayne and Mike, though, he hadn't made me feel smothered.

Instead, I'd felt protected, and possibly cherished.

To be honest, it was kind of a good problem to have.

We were tidying up the bar before it opened one night when I turned to watch him. He was standing by the bottles taking inventory and I was wiping down tables and counters. I watched the way he checked to make sure we had enough of everything we needed that night, and then I realized something.

This was the man I wanted to stay with.

It wasn't this big, overwhelming feeling or this rushing decision. It wasn't like a bunch of doves flew out from behind me when I made this choice.

It was more like, I was watching him and I knew that he was kind and goodhearted and passionate, and I liked those things.

And I wanted more.

Setting down my washcloth, I made my way over to him. He didn't look until I was almost behind him. I placed my hand on his lower back and he turned to me and smiled.

"Hello, my pretty tiger."

And that was it.

I was done for.

"I love you," I told him. I wasn't sure how I was supposed to feel when I said something like that, but the emotion I felt most strongly was *peace*.

He looked at me for only a moment before a grin slid over his own face.

"I love you more," he murmured, and then he kissed me.

Kapono didn't hold back. He just stopped what he was doing, pulled me into his arms, and pressed his lips over mine.

I knew in that moment that I wasn't going to run. I'd been debating with myself, unsure of what the right move was going to be, but right then, I knew. I knew I was going to stay. I knew it was the decision that made the most sense, and I knew that no matter what came next, Kapono was going to be by my side.

When he pulled back, he cupped my face.

"I don't even know what I was doing before you walked into my life."

"I didn't even know I needed you until I met you," I admitted quietly. It was a little embarrassing to say, to admit to being lost, but there it was.

Before I could say anything else, he lifted me up and placed me on the bar. He positioned himself between my legs and placed his hands on my thighs. I was wearing a skirt, which meant everything had gone riding up when he'd placed me so high on the counter, but Kapono didn't mind. He liked it.

"Marry me for real," he whispered.

"What?"

"Marry me," he smiled. "For real."

"Kapono...are you sure?"

It wasn't what I was supposed to say. I was supposed to say yes, and I was supposed to start crying, but all I could ask was whether this was for real.

Whether this was the thing that was really going to shape our future.

"Marry me, Darla," he whispered, and I nodded.

"Okay, Kapono. I will marry you."

22

Kapono

I pushed her legs apart and moved her skirt up, so it bunched around her waist. I was finally going to marry the woman of my dreams, and that meant we needed to celebrate. Now. This wasn't a celebration that could wait days or weeks. I needed her now. Even waiting another hour was going to be impossible.

"What...what are you doing?"

Her breath was like a whisper as I smiled up at her.

"Celebrating," I told her honestly.

We had a lot to celebrate. We'd met each other. We'd fallen for each other.

And now, we were about to embark on an incredible life together.

I was under no impression that I was bad for Darla. I was good for her. She was good for me, too. In the past, my relationships had been short-lived and fueled by immaturity, but this relationship was different.

My mother had told me about the luck of the shifters. It was believed that every shifter had one true mate they were supposed to find and fall in love with, and I'd gotten that in Darla. I hadn't talked with her about it, but I knew that she felt it just as I did.

Now, I leaned down and started savoring her. I tasted her. She threw her head back and closed her eyes. She didn't care that we were in the middle of the bar, and I didn't care either.

Nobody was going to catch us, and even if they did, it didn't matter.

The only thing that mattered was making her fall apart right here, right now.

"Kapono..."

I would never get tired of my name on her lips.

I would never get worn out.

Never get exhausted.

I would do this forever if she would come for me.

The sweet scent of her arousal filled the bar as I tasted her over and over again. Everyone who came in tonight would know what we'd done, but I didn't care at all. The only thing that mattered to me was getting her to experience this moment, getting her to feel everything I was feeling and more.

"Come for me," I looked up at her.

Rising back up, I kissed her as my hand found its way between her legs. I kissed her as she groaned and wiggled right there on the counter. I didn't stop touching her until her body tensed and then shuddered as waves of pleasure claimed her consciousness.

Oh, she was so perfect.

And I didn't deserve her.

*

An hour later, the two of us were busy making drinks when one of the regulars, Bagel, plopped down at the end of the bar.

"Good evening."

"Good to see you," Darla grinned. She reached for a bottle of whipped vodka. "The regular?"

Bagel nodded and waited while she added sprite with extra ice and the slightest dash of whipped vodka. Bagel didn't like strong drinks and I never charged him for what he enjoyed while at the bar. He tipped like crazy, though, so he was good in my book.

Darla set the drink down, and Bagel smiled.

"Thank you!" He pulled out a newspaper he'd been carrying and set it down on the bar counter. Then he tapped it.

"Good picture of you," he said to Darla. "You look absolutely lovely."

"What?" Darla turned toward Bagel. "What are you talking about?" As far as I knew, neither one of us had any reason to have our picture in the newspaper.

"Your picture," he smiled, turning the paper around. "In your wedding announcement."

Darla looked like she was going to throw up, and my own stomach churned. No. This couldn't have been how they found her.

Could it have?

Wedding announcement?

It had to be my mom. She must have submitted an announcement for the paper because she was so happy for us. We'd asked her not to post on social media, and she'd listened. She'd abided by our "no social media" rule, but this was different.

This was a damn *newspaper*.

Only people in Rawr County would be able to see the picture, right? Darla looked sick as I reached for the newspaper to read the title. Sure enough, it was the local paper, which meant it wouldn't have been distributed outside of the county.

But Dwayne and Mike were in Rawr County.

And I was guessing they'd seen the picture.

23

Darla

Usually when he looked at me, it was like time stood still.

My heart always seemed to stop beating, I held my breath, and I just *existed*.

And nothing else in the world mattered.

Nothing.

That was something I'd only ever heard about in books. I'd heard these stories that people had experienced: tales of people falling in love. Stories where everyone gets a happy ending.

And as a kid, I used to love that stuff. I *loved* the fact that sometimes, people got these deliciously happy endings and these beautiful love stories. I loved that.

For a very, very brief moment in time, I was starting to think that I was going to get all of those things, too.

And for a very brief moment in time, I'd allowed myself to believe I was worthy of him.

Only now, things were different.

They were different because this was about me and him and us.

And there was a threat to all of this. Something was dangerous. Something was threatening our way of life.

Someone.

Two someone's.

I stared at Bagel and I felt like I had been punched. It was like all of the air had been sucked out my lungs and this experience, this life that was supposed to be so wonderful between me and Kapono, it had just been destroyed.

Our picture was in the newspaper.

Kapono grabbed me and hauled me into the back room.

"Are you okay?"

Not really.

I suddenly felt scared.

Afraid.

Anxious.

Suddenly, it was like none of our hard work mattered because she'd found us.

"I thought we asked your mother not to share pictures of us on social media," I pointed out. My voice quivered just a little. I had really thought that we were going to be okay. I'd managed to somewhat convince myself that Dwayne and Mike wouldn't be back...that even if they were the ones who had come to see Kapono, that they wouldn't return.

"Social media," he sighed. "But we didn't say no newspaper announcements," he frowned. "That's where this is coming from."

I understood. Really, I did. And it was an honor to be marrying someone as kindhearted and wonderful as Kapono.

Even though the announcement was about our wedding, and it hadn't actually taken place yet, I was honored. No, I was delighted. The two of us were going to have a wonderful private ceremony at some point. We wouldn't tell anyone. It would just be us.

And it would be everything we'd ever wanted..

Everything we'd ever hoped for.

And more.

But we had to stay alive.

And I had to stay here.

And I had to get rid of my terrible past that just kept seem to keep chasing me.

No matter how much I ran, they kept coming back, and I hated how very scared I felt at this thought.

"I know your mom was just trying to be kind," I admitted to him.

I knew that she was trying to do what was best for her son.

"She misses my brother," Kapono said gently.. I knew it couldn't have been easy. that was how I'd feel, too, if I was the one missing someone I loved.

"I know she does."

"I miss him, too. I just know he would have adored you," Kapono told me.

"He sounds like a great guy."

"He was," he said, "but unfortunately, your picture is out there now."

"Not yours," I pointed out. "They might not realize that you and I are together." The picture that had been printed featured me looking at the camera. My arms were wrapped around Kapono, but his back was to the photographer, his mother. Anyone looking at the picture would see me grinning, but unless they'd already met my mate, they wouldn't know it was him.

"When one of them came into the bar," Kapono said slowly, "he didn't know I knew you. He must have seen the picture and known that you were in the area, but he didn't know where."

"That's bad," I sighed. "What if he went to other places?"

"He might have," Kapono admitted. Other shifters who were excited to share the news might have given him some information. Then again, maybe not. Shifters tended to protect their own, and most of us could scent a human.

This was something I'd only just started learning. When I'd first started, I hadn't been able to distinguish between the different scents.

I could now.

I could do a lot of things now, and I had Kapono to thank for that. He was a good teacher. I wasn't sure if he did it on purpose or not, but he was very, very good at guiding me.

And he was the one who had really helped me learn to control things like my nose and my scenting abilities.

Despite the fact that the two of us were getting married, I was going to have to spend a lot of time thanking him for everything he'd done.

I knew that I would never really be able to pay him back, but I could try.

I was willing to spend the rest of my life making it up to him if I had to.

"We're going to be okay," Kapono said. "If they find you, I'll fight for you, Darla."

And I knew that it was true.

24

Kapono

It was close to the end of the night when they came back. The bar was nearly empty. Sloan was cleaning up, Brock had gone home for the night, and Bagel was sitting at one end of the counter with his back to the front door. He always set on the end of the bar that was closest to the front door. I never asked why, and nobody ever took Bagel's spot.

Now, they were here.

The captors.

The *magicians*.

Even though I'd been expecting it, and even though I knew that we would have to face these bastards, it didn't make things any easier.

Darla was my mate.

I'd accepted that.

Craved it.

Needed it.

She was the woman I was going to spend my entire future with, which meant I needed to make sure that I was guarding and protecting that future even if I didn't want to fight these guys.

It was both of them who walked into the bar this time, and I wasn't sure what their problem was or why they thought wandering into this place was a good idea.

Maybe they didn't know we were all shifters here.

That *had* to be it.

There was no other reasonable, logical explanation for the fact that they were just prancing in. I spotted them right away, and so did Darla.

So did Sloan.

So did Bagel.

Jim and Kellan were both gone, but I had enough people here with me that I knew I'd be okay without any additional assistance. It was a tiny crowd, to be sure, but people always underestimated Sloan. She might have been somewhat small for a shifter, but she was fierce and strong.

Besides, Sloan didn't put up with shit from anyone.

The taller man walked up to the bar and dropped his keys on it. I just *knew* they were going to scratch my perfect counter, but I'd polish it later. I wiped all traces of irritation from my face as I looked up at him.

Here was the man who had hurt my mate.

"What?" I asked. I wanted to punch him in the face. It took every ounce of self-control not to do that because there was still a chance they'd go away, and there was still a chance I wouldn't have to do what I thought I was going to do.

Suddenly, all of the stories about people making these obscenely terrible choices when it came to dealing with their mates made sense. I'd heard so many stories about people fighting and hurting and *killing* people because they crossed someone's mate.

I hadn't understood it before, but I did now.

I did now.

The tall man at the counter spoke with the slightest hint of annoyance in his voice. It sounded like he didn't want to be here anymore than I wanted him here. Unfortunately for him, that wasn't going to be enough to save him.

"Remember me? I was here earlier."

How could I forget?

Darla was smart. She quickly slipped into the back room of the bar before the guy noticed her. I knew that she didn't want to fight, but I was more than ready. The urge to run to her and kiss her and tell her that he wasn't going to hurt her overwhelmed me, but I still didn't know what I was supposed to do right now.

Grant would have known.

That had always been one of the best things about my brother. He'd always know exactly how to approach different situations and he'd never been shy when it came to dealing with anything hard.

"What do you want?" I repeated. I wasn't going to let him know that I remembered or that I knew who he was. His friend was walking around, obviously casing the place. He wasn't being even the slightest bit discreet, which was particularly annoying.

He could have at least *pretended* to be interested in drinking.

Instead, Asshole Number Two was walking around checking the exits and windows. Bagel was still sitting at the end of the bar and shot me a look that said, "You want me to punch him?"

It was a strange thing, facing my future wife's abusers. These two men had tormented her for years and they were obviously lost without her. Apparently, she really had been the star of their show. Why else would they care so much about finding her?

If they hadn't actually *needed* her, they would have let her go. Here they were, though, hunting her down. It was like they were latched onto her scent and they weren't willing to let go.

It was like they would *never* let go.

"I'm looking for a woman," the man said.

"So, I heard."

"She's my girlfriend."

A lie.

"She ran off with our kid."

What?

Another lie.

Stupid lie, too.

Darla didn't have children. She never had. She'd be damn gorgeous as a pregnant woman with a full, round belly. I'd love to have her grow our cubs one day. Maybe one day soon.

She hadn't had this dude's baby, though.

Even if he didn't reek of lies, the reality was that she simply had never given birth.

"Unfortunate," I shrugged. If he left quietly and never came back, then maybe that would be the end of it. Only, I knew that it would never be over.

As long as these guys were out there, Darla would never be safe. She'd never find peace. She'd never be able to relax because they were here.

It was the end of the night, so Bagel was the only customer left. He was hanging out because he didn't want to go home alone, and since we'd just been getting ready to clean, I was in no hurry to push him out.

I wanted to turn and run to Darla, to promise her that everything was going to be all right. I could *scent* her anguish from the back room, and I was just glad that she'd gone and hid.

Later, she would probably feel upset about her decision to hide. Later, she'd wish that she had faced her abusers, but I didn't care about that.

"I know she's here," the man's eyes narrowed.

And that was it.

That was the moment my patience snapped.

That was the moment I realized that I no longer had a choice. Simply *hoping* he was going to leave wasn't going to work. Instead, I had to force him to vanish.

I thrust my hand out and grabbed him by the throat before I could stop myself.

"You must be Dwayne," I guessed. His eyes widened, so I knew I was right.

"He's got ribbons coming out of his pockets," Bagel said, confused. I could hear the lingering question in the tone of his voice: *"Who the hell is this guy?"*

"He's a magician of sorts," I offered. Mike, his accomplice, suddenly noticed what was happening.

"Hey!" Mike yelled. "Let him go!" He started to hurry over, but Sloan slipped between a couple of tables and scurried over to him. Then she grabbed him by the back of the neck. She looked small and petite, but she had the strength of multiple men. She wasn't human, but she definitely looked it. People were always underestimating her.

"Not so fast," Sloan said. "Boss, what's the deal with these guys?"

I was still gripping Dwayne's throat.

"They hurt Darla," I said.

"Oh," Sloan shrugged. "Is that so?"

"She's ours," the guy I was holding by the neck managed to grasp out. "She's ours."

Sloan looked to me for permission, and I nodded subtly before they realized what was happening. Sloan and I both shifted our hands into our tiger paws just long enough for our sharp claws to come out. The men were dead before they hit the ground. Their blood started spilling out on the floor, and then it was over.

We'd done it.

It may not have been the best way to deal with the problem, but it was definitely an effective one.

"What the fuck?" Bagel looked shocked. He looked up at me. "What the fuck?"

"Nobody messes with the boss' wife," Sloan shrugged. Sloan was completely unbothered by the fact that we'd just killed two men in the middle of my bar. Sloan was a tough shifter. I didn't know her entire story, but I knew that she didn't put up with crap from anyone.

She'd killed before, and she'd probably do it again, but I didn't care.

I needed people like her here in the bar.

"Bagel, you going to help me clean up or what?" Sloan asked, gesturing to the mess on the floor.

Bagel's jaw dropped. He was only *barely* drinking, which meant he was pretty close to sober, but I had a feeling he'd need a stiff drink after all of this.

"Are you seriously asking me to clean up a body?"

"Yes," Sloan said.

"Why would I do that?"

Sloan put her hands on her hips. "Because if you don't, I'm going to tell Kapono that we're sleeping together, and we both know he doesn't like me fucking his customers."

That got Bagel moving, even though he was muttering about the fact that she'd just outed them. I ignored them both because I didn't really care and it wasn't any of my business. Besides, I'd had an inkling about the two of them, anyway.

Then I turned to head to the backroom.

"Darla?" I called out, opening the heavy wooden door. The scent of sadness and fear was still strong, but she was going to be okay. Everything was going to be totally fine.

She was in my arms before I even stepped inside. She was crying, but she threw her arms around me tightly.

"I'm sorry I ran. I'm so weak. I was scared."

"No," I shook my head as I held her. "You're not weak."

I would never use those words to describe this woman. I loved her far too much to allow her to talk about herself like that.

She wasn't weak.

She was incredible.

There were a lot of things in the world that didn't make sense to me, but Darla did. She was the sunshine in my life and the light in my heart. She was the kindest, sweetest, most interesting person I'd ever met, and I had literally just killed for her.

And I didn't care.

I didn't care that the world was now short two shitty magicians.

I didn't care that the magic show would be cancelled.

I didn't care that I'd ended someone's life and that Sloan had helped me.

I'd give her a raise and we'd never speak of this again. The only thing that mattered was Darla. I needed her to be safe.

"You're going to get in trouble," she whispered. "I'll tell everyone it was me. Don't worry. I'll tell them it was me."

"No," I pulled back and lifted her chin. "We'll tell no one."

"What?"

"Shifters have our own way of handling things, love. Nobody is going to ask question. Bagel's got some land. He'll make them disappear for good."

"What are you saying?"

"I'm saying there's a reason Bagel doesn't pay for drinks, love, and there's a reason that shifters live in groups."

"Safety in numbers," she realized, and I nodded.

It was probably a weird thing for her to finally realize, and it was certainly a weird thing to suddenly bring up, but yes, shifters tended to live together because we had to protect ourselves. Shifters tended to exist slightly outside of the law. Although there were some human laws that we followed and respected, everyone knew that if you messed with a shifter, you might disappear.

Nobody asked too many questions about it.

"You're safe now," I promised Darla, and it was a promise I planned to keep for an eternity. She was safe, and nothing bad was ever going to happen to her again. I would go to the ends of the Earth to protect her, and I knew that she was going to do the same for me.

She was wonderful, and she was perfect, and she truly was my mate.

I never planned on letting her go.

Ever.

Epilogue

Cosmo
Three months later

The wedding reception of Kapono and Darla was supposed to be a lovely affair, and to be honest, it was.

Kapono's business partner, Jim, had fully finished designing the basement of the bar and had transported it into the most majestic space I'd ever seen - primarily because there were inexpensive drinks and lots and lots of games.

The arcade games that filled the basement ranged from things I'd played as a kid to games I'd never even heard of, but it was really quite fantastic, and I was so very delighted with it.

Or at least, I should have been.

I should have been delighted.

It was hard to celebrate with Kapono and Darla when my own heart was filled with so much longing that it hurt. The woman of my dreams was someone I'd never be able to really have.

And that realization did more than sting.

It actually, physically hurt.

It should have been illegal for her to look that good.

There she was, walking into the room like she owned the place, and I was nothing more than the schmuck she worked for.

Those stupidly tall heels with the pencil skirts and the carefully pressed blouses were going to be my undoing.

I knew it.

I'd thought for years that she was my mate, but I'd also thought that she was far too good for a dumbass like me.

And now it was too late.

She'd started seeing someone.

It had been subtle at first. The little indicators that she had a lover had slowly permeated the office, though, and I hadn't known what to do.

The flowers that appeared here and there weren't supposed to be gifts from a man.

Not unless that man was me.

Tonight, though, she wasn't with a man. She was here alone. She noticed me staring at her and she smiled almost shyly.

"You could take a picture," she teased. "It'll last longer."

But I already knew that because I had so many pictures of her. She was everything to me, and I was...

Not worthy.

Read Cosmo's story in SHIFTERS OF RAWR COUNTY: BOOK SIX.

If you enjoyed reading about Savannah, there's an entire series for you that takes place in Honeypot, Colorado! Read Honeypot Darlings by Sophie Stern. Savannah's story appears in book two: The Bear's Virgin Mate.

Author

Sophie Stern writes vampires, cowboys, werewolves, dragons, and fairy tales. Her books feature deliciously wonderful characters and deliciously naughty adventures. If you enjoyed *The Polar Bear's Fake Mate*, you may like one of her other romances, such as *Dark Favors* or *The Feisty Librarian*.
Of course, you'll also want to check out another story that takes place in Rawr County: The Dragon's Christmas Treasure. Please make sure you subscribe to Sophie's mailing list *here*[1].
You can also follow her on Facebook[2] for frequent updates.
Thank you so much for reading.

---

1. http://eepurl.com/bh8v_j

2. http://www.facebook.com/sexysophiestern/

Books

Other books by Sophie Stern
HONEYPOT DARLINGS
HONEYPOT BABIES
DRAGON ISLE
THE FABLESTONE CLAN
THE FEISTY DRAGONS
DRAGON ENCHANTED
DON'T DATE DEMONS
POLAR BEARS OF THE AIR FORCE
DARK FAVORS
SAVORED

Sophie's books are available wherever eBooks are sold.

If you enjoyed this story, check out these other books by Sophie Stern!

*

CONQUERED (The Hidden Planet)

Abducted.

Taken.

Locked away.

Fiona doesn't know true fear until she is whisked away from her loving family and doting boyfriend. When she finds herself on an alien ship with only a gHankt beast for company, her fear turns to anger when she realizes her loved ones have betrayed her.

Quinn doesn't know what to do with the squirrely little human aboard his ship. Yeah, he bought her, but only to save her from a worse fate. She has no idea what could have happened to her if he hadn't found her. She has no idea what could have happened on Dreagle. But now she's on his ship and somehow, she's wormed her way into his heart. Can he ever let her go?

CONQUERED is available wherever eBooks are sold.

ALIEN BEAST

He's a war hero.
She's a virgin.
He's broken.
She's perfect.

When he finds her in the midst of an alien war, Luke takes Willow for himself. He can't help himself. He's never taken a prisoner alive before, but Willow is different. He needs her. He wants her. Most of all, he craves her.

Willow is a human who has the worst luck in the world. When the tour ship she's on malfunctions and crash-lands on the wrong planet, she's thrust into the middle of a war: one she has no desire to be in.

Then everything changes.

She's captured by an alien beast unlike anything she's ever seen before.

And the worst part is that after awhile, she's not so sure she wants him to let her go.

ALIEN BEAST is available wherever eBooks are sold.

STARBOARD

Christina hasn't had a regular Dom since her husband died in Afghanistan. She's a war widow with a daughter: she doesn't have time for relationships, but she does make time to play.

Christina goes to Anchored to unwind and to have her submissive needs met. Whether she's playing with a Dom or Domme, Christina's partners all know one thing: she's there to serve, not to find love.

It's all fun and games for the Damsel of the Dungeon until a new Dom arrives and he sets his sights on her.

Only, he's not just interested in scening with Christina.

He's interested in everything.

Zack has always considered himself a good lawyer, a loyal friend, and an observant Dominant. When his business partner and best friend, Tony, invites him to visit a local sex club, Zack's ready for anything.

Except the feisty brunette who doesn't want to be taken care of.

After the third time he sees Christina refusing aftercare, Zack decides to do something about it, only Christina isn't like other subs.

It's a good thing he loves a challenge.

*

CHAPTER ONE

Christina

"Are you ready?" Odessa's shoes click loudly as she makes her way across the locker room floor. She's wearing five-inch bright-red stilettos tonight and honestly, I have no idea how the hell she manages to walk in those things. I prefer to be barefoot, myself, but that's probably just because I don't have half the grace Odessa has.

"Just about," I tell her. "Let me finish my mascara." I twirl the mascara brush over my eyelashes one last time. I really should invest in falsies, but I'm just not confident enough in my ability to put them on. Besides, the double-dark mascara I'm wearing tonight makes me look incredible.

Kissable.

Fuckable.

It makes me look unstoppable.

"You look great, love," Odessa kisses me on the cheek and manages to pry me away from the vanity mirror. "But it's time. The night is in full swing and if I'm not mistaken, you have a date with Destiny tonight."

"Her name is Mistress D," I smile, but Odessa is right. We both know Destiny from outside the club. It should make playing together a little weird, but somehow, it doesn't. Somehow, playing with Mistress D is different than working with Destiny.

Odessa just rolls her eyes and gives me a once over. She reaches out and adjusts the corset I'm wearing, pushing my breasts up just a little higher. Then she walks around me, smoothing out the miniskirt I'm wearing and making sure each part of my outfit looks good, perfect. She makes sure I look complete, and for that, I am grateful.

I've been playing at Anchored for months now, but sometimes, I still get nervous. Tonight isn't my first night playing with Mistress D and it certainly won't be my last, but sometimes I still worry that I'm not going to be good enough to please my partners. Sometimes I worry that I'm not going to be good enough to make this fun for them.

"Stop over-thinking," Odessa warns me sternly. "Stay focused on the scene. Remember, Christina: stay focused."

"I will."

She grabs my chin and turns me toward her. Odessa's bright brown eyes practically glow as she gazes at me.

"You are not a mother tonight. You are not a widow. You are not a childcare provider. You are not anything but a submissive. Do you understand?"

"I understand."

"Say it for me, love."

"I am only a submissive tonight."

"That's right," Odessa nods, seemingly satisfied. "Don't make the mistake of spacing off during your scene, okay?"

I blush, embarrassed she remembers the debacle from a few weeks ago. I had been playing with someone new and just couldn't really get into the submissive mindset. As a result, I was spacing off, thinking about grocery lists and errands, and the scene fell short.

Really short.

"I won't space off tonight," I tell her. Odessa is a submissive, too, and she's going to be playing with her regular Dom tonight. Theodore is a kind-hearted tax-attorney who is seriously cut. He's huge, and if I was at the end of his whip, I'd be terrified.

Odessa isn't, though. She loves it, takes it in stride. She's a perfect fit for him and sometimes, I wonder why the two of them aren't dating.

"Good girl," Odessa says, pressing a kiss to my cheek. I give her the same once-over she gave me, fixing her top and adjusting her boy-shorts to make sure every part of her looks perfect. We each take one last look in the mirror, but then it's time.

It's time to leave the safety of the locker room.

It's time to go to Anchored.

Odessa takes my hand and we leave the room together. Instantly, the sound of the heavy music hits our ears, reminding us where we are. Tonight is about fun and excitement. It's about relaxing. It's about unwinding, but it's about more than that, too: it's about submission.

Tonight is about giving ourselves to our partners, and in return, they'll give us a little bit of themselves, as well. That's the true beauty of submission. In giving of myself, I get something in return. The feeling of offering myself to my partner is satisfying in and of itself, but knowing that it meets my partner's needs, as well, is even more fantastic.

I like knowing that my Dom or Domme feels good about themselves when we're through playing together.

I like knowing that they're having just as much fun as me.

And I like that at the end of the night, when I walk out of Anchored, I'm leaving them at the door.

It's fucked up, but I don't really care.

Anchored is my release. It's my safe space. It's my haven. Anchored is where I go because I have nowhere else to go. Anchored is the only time I get to myself, and I take it. It's the only time I have away from my daughter. It's the only time I can be me.

I'm not the best mother in the world. I certainly wasn't the best wife. When Cameron died, he left me alone. He left me without anyone in the world. Even now, I don't have anyone. It's been two damn years since he died and I have no one.

No one.

But I have Anchored.

I have this place where I can forget, for just a couple of hours, that I've lost my true love.

I have this place where I can forget, for just a little while, that my life fell apart and I'm only starting to rebuild it.

I have this place where I can forget, for just a tiny bit of time, that I am completely alone in this world.

I have this place.

And I'm not giving it up.

I'm not going to get in a relationship with one of my play partners only to have us break up. Then coming to the club would be awkward, weird, and uncomfortable. I'm not going to get into a relationship where we have a fight, and then neither one of us goes to the club. I'm not interested in that.

I don't want to sacrifice my safe space for the temporary satisfaction of being someone's romantic partner. That's not what I want and it's certainly not what I need. That's not for me.

So at the end of the night, after I play with Mistress D, I'll spend some time crying in the locker room showers. I'll wash my hair. I'll clean my face. And then I'll get dressed, get in my car, and go back to the real world, where I am a mother, and a childcare worker, and a widow.

I'll go back to the real world where everything hurts.
I'll go back to my life as a solitary person.
I'll go back to my world.

"Christina," I hear a sharp, crisp voice, and I turn. A tall black woman with braids tumbling past her shoulders is walking toward me. A corset pushes her breasts up and out. She's wearing tight leather pants and stilettos that are even taller than Odessa's.

Instantly, I drop to my knees, palms down. I bow my head and I wait quietly for my Domme of the night to tell me how I've done so far. I wait until she tells me it's time. I wait until she tells me she's ready.

And when Mistress D tells me I look beautiful, and that she's ready to play with me, I take her hand, and I walk into the world of Anchored.

Want to read more?
Get your copy wherever eBooks are sold!

Don't miss out!

Visit the website below and you can sign up to receive emails whenever Sophie Stern publishes a new book. There's no charge and no obligation.

https://books2read.com/r/B-A-XOYC-SLDYB

BOOKS 2 READ

Connecting independent readers to independent writers.

Also by Sophie Stern

Alien Chaos
Destroyed
Guarded
Saved
Christmas on Chaos
Alien Chaos: A Sci-Fi Alien Romance Bundle

Aliens of Malum
Deceived: An Alien Brides Romance
Betrayed: An Alien Brides Romance
Fallen: An Alien Brides Romance
Captured: An Alien Brides Romance
Regret
Crazed
For Keeps
Rotten: An Alien Brides Romance

Anchored
Starboard
Battleship
All Aboard
Abandon Ship
Below Deck
Crossing the Line
Anchored: Books 1-3
Anchored: Books 4-6

Ashton Sweets
Christmas Sugar Rush
Valentine's Sugar Rush
St. Patty's Sugar Rush
Halloween Sugar Rush

Bullies of Crescent Academy
You Suck
Troublemaker
Jaded

Club Kitten Dancers
Move

Pose
Climb

Dragon Enchanted
Hidden Mage
Hidden Captive
Hidden Curse

Dragon Isle
The Dragon Fighter
A Dragon's Bite
Lost to the Dragon
Beware of Dragons
Cowboy Dragon
Dark Heart of the Dragon
Once Upon a Dragon
Catching the Dragon

Fate High School
You Wish: A High School Reverse Harem Romance
Freak: A Reverse Harem High School Romance
Get Lost: A Reverse Harem Romance

Good Boys and Millionaires
Good Boys and Millionaires 1
Good Boys and Millionaires 2

Grimalkin Needs Brides
Ekpen (Intergalactic Dating Agency)

Honeypot Babies
The Polar Bear's Baby
The Jaguar's Baby
The Tiger's Baby

Honeypot Darlings
The Bear's Virgin Darling
The Bear's Virgin Mate
The Bear's Virgin Bride

Office Gentlemen
Ben From Accounting

Polar Bears of the Air Force
Staff Sergeant Polar Bear
Master Sergeant Polar Bear
Airman Polar Bear
Senior Airman Polar Bear

Red
Red: Into the Dark
Red: Through the Dark
Red: Beyond the Dark

Return to Dragon Isle
Dragons Are Forever
Dragon Crushed: An Enemies-to-Lovers Paranormal Romance
Dragon's Hex
Dragon's Gain
Dragon's Rush: An Enemies-to-Lovers Paranormal Romance

Shifters at Law
Wolf Case
Bearly Legal
Tiger Clause
Sergeant Bear

Dragon Law

Shifters of Rawr County
The Polar Bear's Fake Mate
The Lion's Fake Wife
The Tiger's Fake Date
The Wolf's Pretend Mate
The Tiger's Pretend Husband
The Dragon's Fake Fiancée

Stormy Mountain Bears
The Lumberjack's Baby Bear
The Writer's Baby Bear
The Mountain Man's Baby Bears

Sweet Nightmares
The Vampire's Melody
The Sound of Roses

Team Shifter
Bears VS Wolves
No Fox Given

The Fablestone Clan
Dragon's Oath
Dragon's Breath
Dragon's Darling
Dragon's Whisper
Dragon's Magic

The Feisty Dragons
Untamed Dragon
Naughty Dragon
Monster Dragon

The Hidden Planet
Vanquished
Outlaw
Conquered

The Wolfe City Pack
The Wolf's Darling
The Wolf's Mate
The Wolf's Bride

Standalone
Saucy Devil
Billionaire on Top
Jurassic Submissive
The Editor
Alien Beast
Snow White and the Wolves
Kissing the Billionaire
Wild
Alien Dragon
The Royal Her
Be My Tiger
Alien Monster
The Luck of the Wolves
Honeypot Babies Omnibus Edition
Honeypot Darlings: Omnibus Edition
Red: The Complete Trilogy
The Swan's Mate
The Feisty Librarian
Polar Bears of the Air Force
Wild Goose Chase
Star Princess
The Virgin and the Lumberjacks
Resting Bear Face
I Dare You, King
Shifters at Law
Pretty Little Fairies
Seized by the Dragon

The Fablestone Clan: A Paranormal Dragon-Shifter Romance Collection
Star Kissed
Big Bad Academy
Club Kitten Omnibus
Stormy Mountain Bears: The Complete Collection
Bitten by the Vampires
Beautiful Villain
Dark Favors
Savored
Vampire Kiss
Chaotic Wild: A Vampire Romance
Bitten
Heartless
The Dragon's Christmas Treasure
Out of the Woods
Bullies of Crescent Academy
Craving You: A Contemporary Romance Collection
Chasing Whiskey
The Hidden Planet Trilogy
The Bratty Dom
Tokyo Wolf
The Single Dad Who Stole My Heart
Free For Him
The Feline Gaze
Fate High School
Dragon Beast: A Beauty and the Beast Retelling
Boulder Bear
Megan Slays Vampires
Once Upon a Shift: A Paranormal Romantic Comedy

Made in the USA
Columbia, SC
15 January 2025